She tugged at his emotions in a way he hadn't expected.

If he'd had any sense, John would have taken up a position in the hall to protect her. Instead, he dropped down into the easy chair across from her and stared at her broodingly. What was he going to do about Elizabeth? She was his boss and the last woman on earth he should even be thinking about kissing. But there it was, like it or not. All he could think about was carrying her upstairs to bed and driving them both crazy, and he didn't have a clue what he was going to do about it.

The only thing he did know for sure was that he wasn't leaving her unprotected. If he had to sit and watch her all night in order to keep her safe, then that's what he was going to do.

Dear Reader,

Under His Protection is about Elizabeth Wyatt, who stays at the Broken Arrow Ranch while her brother and his new wife are on their honeymoon, and it was great fun to write. Elizabeth is a woman with spunk, and when she meets John Cassidy, the new ranch foreman, the fur flies. They each think they're in charge, when in reality, neither stands a chance against Fate. A battle of wills turns into a fight for love and happily-ever-after, and in the end, they both win. Life doesn't get any better than that.

Enjoy!

Linda Turner

UNDER HIS PROTECTION

Linda Turner

Romantic
SUSPENSE

ISBN-13: 978-0-373-27566-3
ISBN-10: 0-373-27566-8

UNDER HIS PROTECTION

This edition published by arrangement with Harlequin Books S.A.

Visit Silhouette Books at www.eHarlequin.com

Printed in U.S.A.

Books by Linda Turner

Silhouette Romantic Suspense

‡*Gable's Lady* #523
‡*Cooper* #553
‡*Flynn* #572
‡*Kat* #590
Who's the Boss? #649
The Loner #673
Maddy Lawrence's Big Adventure #709
The Lady in Red #763
†*I'm Having Your Baby?!* #799
†*A Marriage-Minded Man?* #829
†*The Proposal* #847
†*Christmas Lone-Star Style* #895
****The Lady's Man** #931
***A Ranching Man* #992
***The Best Man* #1010
***Never Been Kissed* #1051
The Enemy's Daughter #1064
The Man Who Would Be King #1124
***Always a McBride* #1231
††*Deadly Exposure* #1304
††*Beneath the Surface* #1321
††*A Younger Man* #1423
††*Mission: M.D.* #1456
**Fortune Hunter's Hero* #1473
**Under His Protection* #1496

‡The Wild West
†The Lone Star Social Club
**Those Marrying McBrides!
††Turning Points
*Broken Arrow Ranch

LINDA TURNER

began reading romances in high school and began writing them one night when she had nothing else to read. She's been writing ever since. Single and living in Texas, she travels every chance she gets, scouting locales for her books.

Prologue

"You're getting married?"

"When?"

"You can't! We haven't even met Rainey yet!"

"You'll get your chance when you come for the wedding," Buck said with a chuckle. "The wedding's a week from Saturday."

Dropping that little tidbit of information into the four-way transcontinental conference call to England, Buck watched the clock, counting the seconds as he waited for his sisters' reactions. He didn't have long to wait.

"You can't be serious!" Elizabeth retorted.

"You're darn right he's not serious," Priscilla growled. "That's what? Ten days?"

"No one in their right mind can plan a wedding in ten days," Katherine added. "He's joking."

On the extension, listening to the entire conference call, Rainey laughed softly. "No, he's not. We're getting married a week from Saturday. I know it's short notice, but Buck wanted to get married on your parents' anniversary. So if we don't get married in ten days, we have to wait another year."

"That isn't even an option," Buck growled. "We're not waiting."

"Don't get testy," Elizabeth teased. "No one's asking you to wait."

"Just so we understand each other," he replied. "We want the three of you here for our wedding."

"Then we'd better get off the phone and see about lining up airline tickets," Priscilla said. "I don't even know if my passport's current."

"In a minute," Buck replied. "We need to discuss the honeymoon. Rainey and I are going to Alaska. Who's available to stay at the ranch while we're gone?"

His answer was met with dead silence. "C'mon," he groaned. "You can't do this to me! You can't expect me *not* to go on a honeymoon. One of you has to take my place here at the ranch while I'm gone."

"What ranch?"

"I don't know anything about a ranch."

"Did somebody say something about a ranch?"

Buck grinned. "Cute. Wait until the three of you want to get married. We'll see who's laughing then."

"C'mon, Bucky, don't be that way."

His teeth ground on the hated nickname. "Don't call me that!"

Elizabeth clicked her tongue. "Touchy, touchy."

"You know we're just teasing," Priscilla said. "We'll be there for you."

Despite their teasing, he knew he could count on his sisters. Especially when it came to the Broken Arrow Ranch in Colorado, which the four of them had inherited from their distant American cousin, Hilda Wyatt. The inheritance had come out of the blue. They were the last of the British branch of the Wyatts and had never even met Hilda, the last of the American Wyatts. She'd wanted the ranch to go to family, but the inheritance came with strings. One of them had to always be present at the ranch for twelve months. They could be absent for one night, but not for two in a row, or the deed to the ranch would go to an unnamed heir.

Until now, that hadn't been a problem. Buck had spent the last four months at the ranch without needing any of his sisters to substitute for him, but it hadn't been easy. He'd been harassed and threatened, the ranch had been attacked and vandalized, and Rainey had nearly been killed. He still didn't have a clue who was responsible—it could have been any one of his neighbors or someone in the nearby town of Willow Bend, Colorado—but their motive was painfully clear. If they could scare the Wyatts away from the ranch before the year was out, the ranch would be theirs...if they were the unnamed heir.

"So who's available?" Buck asked. "We're just going to be gone a month."

"A month!" Elizabeth blurted out. "Are you serious?"

"I'm only getting married once, sis. I want us to have a honeymoon we'll remember the rest of our lives."

Elizabeth blinked back tears at his words. Did Rainey have any idea how lucky she was to have found Buck? He was going to make a wonderful husband, a fantastic father, and Elizabeth wasn't surprised that he wanted to do everything in his power to make sure Rainey had a honeymoon she would never forget. He was that kind of man.

For the span of a heartbeat, Elizabeth felt the tug of envy—she hoped the man she married would be as thoughtful as her brother. Then she remembered Spencer and the roses he'd sent her every day for the past four days, a dozen for every week they'd been dating. He, too, was going to make a wonderful husband, she thought with a grin. And he was already talking marriage. Maybe by this time next year…

"So do I have a volunteer or not?" Buck asked. "Surely one of you has some time in your schedule."

Snapping back to attention, Elizabeth didn't hesitate. "I'll do it. Priscilla has a show to prepare for, and Katherine's in a wedding two weeks after yours, so neither of them can stay. That leaves me."

"What about Spencer?" Katherine asked. "Weren't you going to Germany with him for the football tournament?"

"Yes, but he knows about the ranch and the terms of Hilda's will. I have to do my part. He understands that. And since you two are busy and I'm not, it looks like I'll be staying in Colorado for a while."

"I've hired a new foreman," he assured her, "so you don't have to worry about being there by yourself. He's tough. He'll take good care of you."

"I'm sure he will, but I don't want you to worry about me on your honeymoon. I can take care of myself. And if things get really bad, I'll do what I have to to hang onto the ranch, Buck. You can count on me."

He hesitated, then smiled. "I guess I'll see the three of you next week. Don't forget the cowboy boots you bought when you were here last. You're going to need them."

Chapter 1

Ten days later Elizabeth was in no mood for a wedding. She no longer believed in fairy tales, and that's all love was...one big, fat fairy tale that was invented by writers and poets and songwriters. Only a hopeless romantic could actually believe that a man and woman could love each other for a lifetime. She knew better. It only lasted until the love of your life went to Germany for an international soccer tournament and met a blond bimbo.

"You're thinking of Spencer again, aren't you?" Katherine said as she stepped forward to zip her dress for her. "You've got that look on your face..."

Glancing over her shoulder at her, Elizabeth scowled fiercely. "What look? I'm perfectly fine."

"Yeah, right," Priscilla drawled as she stood before the mirror and gave her makeup a last check. "The last time you looked like that, you murdered my doll."

Elizabeth didn't want to laugh, but it gurgled up inside her and escaped before she could stop it. "I did not! You're the one who wanted to see if her head would come off. I just accommodated you."

"*You* put the thought in my head!"

"No, I didn't. It was Katherine."

"It was not!" Katherine objected. "I didn't even know about it until you had the funeral."

Quietly pushing open the door of the bedroom that had been set aside for the bridesmaids' use, Rainey grinned as her soon-to-be sister-in-laws traded quips back and forth. "Buck must have had his hands full, growing up with you three," she told them with a chuckle. "I'm surprised he wasn't part of the beheading."

"Of course he was part of it," Katherine laughed. "He organized the funeral."

"I should have known," Rainey laughed. "That's the man I'm going to marry."

"And have children with," Elizabeth pointed out with a grin. "Are you sure you want to do this?"

Love softened her face and lit up her smile. "Oh, yes. I can't wait!"

Watching her, Elizabeth blinked back tears. She hoped with all her heart that things worked out for Rainey and Buck, but she didn't think she'd ever be able to take that risk herself. Not after the way Spencer had betrayed her. And the way she'd found out! She'd been at Heathrow with her sisters, waiting to board the plane for the States and Buck's wedding, when she'd picked up a copy of one of London's most notorious tabloids. And there on the cover, for all the world to see, was a picture of her boyfriend with a blond bombshell plastered all over him.

Even now she didn't want to believe that he'd cheated on her with some tart who couldn't count to four. But when she'd called him to question him about the picture, he hadn't bothered to deny the fact that he'd taken the woman with him to Germany. He hadn't even understood why she was upset—the woman was nothing but a groupie and didn't mean a thing to him. What was the big deal?

Elizabeth still couldn't believe he'd had the nerve to ask her such a thing. Of course she knew about groupies, how strange women threw themselves at him and his teammates all the time. After all, he was an international soccer star, and she'd seen for herself how he couldn't go anywhere without women he didn't even know flirting with him. She hadn't liked it, but she'd learned to live with it.

The woman in the picture, however, wasn't someone wanting a hug and an autograph. She'd slept with him. He hadn't said as much in so many words, but he hadn't had to. The truth had been right there in the picture, in his eyes, in the blonde's, in the intimate smile they shared.

She shouldn't have been surprised. She'd known in her heart that he was the kind of man who had no use for faithfulness. She'd just convinced herself he loved her enough to change. So much for fairy tales.

"It's going to be okay, Elizabeth," Rainey said quietly, breaking into her thoughts. "You just need some time."

"And another man," Priscilla added, wrinkling her nose at the thought of Spencer. "The best way to get over one man is to get another. Get yourself a cowboy."

"Oh, no!" she said quickly, grimacing. "I don't want a cowboy or anyone else, thank you very much. I'm done with men."

"That's what I said," Rainey told her, grinning. "And now I'm marrying your brother. C'mon. We've got a wedding to go to."

Looping her arm through Elizabeth's, she tugged her out into the hall and laughed as Priscilla and Katherine took positions behind them and gently pushed them down the hall toward the stairs. As the grandfather clock in the front entry struck 8:00 a.m., Rainey laughed. "I can't believe I'm getting married at eight in the morning!"

"What's with that, anyway?" Priscilla asked. "Why so early in the morning?"

"We wanted to start the first day of our marriage as soon as possible," she said simply, grinning as they all spilled into the limo waiting for them in the drive. "So it was either 8:00 a.m. or dawn. We picked 8:00 a.m."

"Thank God!"

Ten minutes later they arrived at the church and Elizabeth fought the need to cry. She loved her brother and Rainey, but she really didn't want to do this. Unfortunately, she couldn't back out without looking like a complete idiot. So she pasted on a smile, and no one knew just how much it cost her as she stepped out of the limo.

Then she walked into the old wood-frame country church that the Wyatt family had attended for over a hundred years, and stopped with a gasp of surprise. If she hadn't known better, she would have sworn she'd stepped back in time.

Although the church had been wired for electricity nearly a hundred years ago, Rainey had chosen to use candles instead. They were everywhere, casting a golden glow over the guests that filled every pew. The sound of violins floated on the hushed, fragrant air, and just that quietly, the ceremony began.

Priscilla started down the aisle, then Katherine. Waiting her turn, Elizabeth was caught off guard by the emotions that tugged at her heart at the sight of her brother waiting at the altar for his bride. Elizabeth liked Rainey, loved her, in fact, but ever since Buck had informed Elizabeth and her sisters that he was getting married, she'd been afraid that he was rushing into a mistake. After all, just last year, he'd been engaged to someone else. But as she watched him smile at Rainey and she caught the look of love that passed between the two of them, she knew that she'd never seen him so happy.

Just that easily, she realized that nothing else mattered. Locking her own heartache away, she started down the aisle, and for the first time since she'd seen the picture of Spencer in the tabloids, the smile that curled the corners of her mouth came straight from her heart.

After that, the morning couldn't have been more magical. Rainey looked like a fairy princess as she started down the aisle toward Buck, and there wasn't a dry eye in the church as they exchanged their *I do's*. Then they rushed up the aisle, glowing with love, and laughingly led their guests back to the ranch for breakfast, then, later in the day, an old-fashioned barbecue and barn dance.

Buck and Rainey had invited not only their friends from both sides of the Atlantic and around the world, but they'd also decided to include the local ranchers and most of the inhabitants of Willow Bend. It was a risky move, but they'd both felt it was better to keep their enemies close at hand than plotting in the shadows, and Elizabeth had to agree with them. If there was anyone there with ulterior motives, they kept them well hidden. Everywhere she looked, people were smiling and laughing and enjoying themselves.

"It's quite a turnout, isn't it? How many do you think are packing guns?"

Surprised, Elizabeth turned to John Cassidy, the Broken Arrow's new foreman. Buck had introduced him to her and her sisters when they arrived the day before yesterday, but there'd been little time to talk to him, let alone get to know him. He'd been busy running the ranch while Buck took care of the last-minute preparations for the wedding and entertained his guests.

And even though Elizabeth had never seen a cowboy, let alone a ranch foreman, before visiting the United States, she had to admit that John Cassidy had the look of a man who could handle just about anything life threw at him. Tall and lean, with a body that was rock hard and a chin that could have been chiseled out of the granite mountains that formed the western boundary of the ranch, he had *tough* written all over him.

And for some reason, that set her teeth on edge. It was the hard glint in his eye, she thought. That *I don't give a damn* look that a lot of women found impossible to resist. She wasn't one of those women.

"I realize I'm not familiar with the local customs," she retorted, "but do people usually bring guns to a wedding in Colorado?"

"That depends on who's getting married and why," he replied dryly. "They've been known to take them to funerals, too."

Not believing that for a second, Elizabeth sniffed, "I wasn't born yesterday, Mr. Cassidy. Just because I was born and raised in England doesn't mean that I don't know a line of bull when I hear it."

"Really?" The corner of his sensuous mouth curling with mocking humor, he lifted a dark male brow at her. "Then maybe you'd care to tell me what that bulge is under your brother's tuxedo jacket?"

"What bulge?" she demanded. "What are you talking about? Buck wouldn't wear a gun to his own wedding!"

"Then he's got a tumor under that jacket," he said. "And so does just about every man here. Didn't you notice? Or did you think we're all nothing but a bunch of hicks in bad suits?"

"No, of course not! I'm not a snob, Mr. Cassidy. I've been too busy circulating to notice how anyone was dressed."

"For your own safety, I suggest you keep your eyes and ears open whenever you're around your neighbors, *Miss* Wyatt. They're not your friends."

"I'm well aware of that," she said stiffly. "I know all about the attacks on the ranch. As far as I'm concerned, my brother and sisters and I can't trust anyone."

"Including me?"

"Including you," she retorted honestly, then graciously added, "At least for now. I know Buck has a great deal of faith in you and that you passed a background check with flying colors. For what it's worth, I hope you do turn out to be as trustworthy as you claim to be. It would be nice to know that there's at least one person outside the family we can trust."

John had to give her credit. He didn't know another woman, short of his mother, who would have looked him right in the eye and given him such a straight answer. "Trust takes time," he said flatly. "Luckily I've got plenty of that."

He had, in fact, nowhere else to go, and he was pretty damn sure that Elizabeth Wyatt knew that. If Buck had told her everything, then she knew that his past was less than stellar. Oh, he'd been a Navy SEAL, and he'd been damn good at it. But then he'd made a mistake—just one—and a man had lost his life.

How many years had he punished himself for that? Three? Five? His commanding officer, the base psychiatrist, even the chaplain, had assured him that everyone made mistakes—it could have happened to anyone. Nothing they'd said, however, had helped. Because he'd killed his best friend, and the memory of that would haunt him for the rest of his life.

He'd tried to forget. But years of drinking hadn't dulled the images from the past—just destroyed his life. His wife had walked out on him, he'd lost his ranch, his self-respect, everything he cared about. And it was all gone forever. When he'd told Elizabeth he had nothing but time, he hadn't lied. He had nowhere else to go, and nothing to do but lose himself in work.

"Just for the record," he added, "I'm not interested in getting my hands on your land. I just want to do the job I was hired to do. That means taking care of the ranch…and you and your sisters when Buck's not here."

For a moment, he didn't think his words registered. Then her sapphire-blue eyes flashed indignantly. "*Take care of me and my sisters?* You think that was the job you were hired to do?"

"I know it's one of them," he retorted. "If you don't believe me, ask Buck."

"Don't worry. I will." Lifting her chin, she stormed off to find her brother.

She found him almost immediately, but it quickly became obvious that she wasn't going to get a chance to talk to him in private. The dancing started, and almost immediately a cowboy asked Elizabeth to dance, grabbed her by the hand and pulled her out onto the dance floor before she could even think to object. Luckily, she'd worn her cowboy boots, just as Buck had suggested. After that, she was on the dance floor for what seemed like hours.

Breathless, she finally escaped with the excuse that she needed something to drink, but then the photographer snagged her and the other bridesmaids and the single women in the crowd so Rainey could throw her bouquet. No one was more surprised than Elizabeth when it fell right into her hands.

"Oh, my God!" she gasped, blanching. "Rainey, you threw that at me deliberately!"

Grinning, she didn't deny it. "You're the oldest. Your turn's next."

"Oh, no, it's not!"

"You'll be married by next year," Priscilla predicted with dancing green eyes.

"I will not. I'm not even dating anyone."

"Doesn't matter," Katherine chuckled. "Everybody knows not to catch a bridal bouquet. Those things are deadly."

Rainey chuckled. "You ain't seen nothing yet. Buck hasn't thrown the garter. Today could be your lucky day."

The words were hardly out of her mouth when Buck threw the garter and hit an eighty-year-old widower right in the chest. The older man had no choice but to catch it.

"That-a-boy, Marlin!" someone in the crowd crowed. "You've been pining for Ludie Morgan all these years. Now she can't say no when you ask her to marry you!"

"Forget Ludie," a cowboy at the back of the crowd advised over the laughter of the crowd. "Elizabeth's prettier!"

Hot color stinging her cheeks, Elizabeth had to laugh. She was saved from having to make a response when Timothy Reynolds, Buck's best man, announced that the bride and groom would soon be leaving for their honeymoon. Friends and family pressed forward, heading for the barn, and as Elizabeth waited with them, she knew that even if she had a chance to talk to Buck for a few minutes, she wouldn't tell him about her problems with John Cassidy. This wasn't the time to burden him with any strife between her and his foreman. And it wasn't as if she couldn't handle the man. She was an owner; he was an employee. End of story.

"Are you sure you can handle everything here by yourself?"

"Maybe we should stay. I could work on my designs here, and Katherine can take some time off from work. Her boss won't mind."

Fighting tears as her sisters tried to talk themselves out of leaving the next morning, Elizabeth hugged them both fiercely. "Don't be silly. You've got your show to work on and Katherine has to be home for Tracy Lawrence's wedding. And you don't need to stay. I'll be fine. Quit worrying."

"Easy for you to say," Katherine retorted. "What if someone tries to kill you the way David Saenz did Rainey?"

"David's dead—"

"So?" Priscilla said. "Somebody hired him to blow up the mine, and whoever it was is pretty damn desperate to drive all of us away so he can get his hands on the ranch. That's the person you need to be worried about. We don't even know who he is!"

"You know I won't take any chances," she replied, hugging them each as the cabby put their luggage in the boot. "And John Cassidy's here. The man's tough as nails. He's not going to let anything happen to me—Buck would have his hide. So quit worrying. I'll be fine."

Katherine and Priscilla looked far from convinced, but the meter was running and they had a flight to catch. "I don't like it," Katherine said huffily. "But I don't know what else we can do about it."

"Watch your back," Priscilla warned. "Don't trust anybody!"

"I won't," she promised, hugging them both one more time. "I'll see you in a month. God, I'm going to miss you!"

"Keep in touch! We expect an e-mail every other day."

"You, too," she said, forcing a bright smile as they slipped into the cab. "I want to know all the little details—where you're going, what you're doing, who you're seeing."

"Oh, no!" Priscilla said with dancing eyes. "I don't kiss and tell!"

Grinning, Katherine pushed her into the cab. "We'll call every Sunday," she told Elizabeth.

"Good. Be careful! I love you."

They waved all the way down the drive, until the cab disappeared around the first curve and they were lost to view.

Later, Elizabeth couldn't say how long she stood

there, staring at the empty drive. Silence enveloped her, broken only by the sigh of the wind as it whispered through the pines. Hugging herself, she was surprised when tears suddenly spilled into her eyes. She'd thought she was prepared for her stay at the ranch. But already she could feel the loneliness creeping in on her, chilling her.

It wouldn't be so bad, she told herself. This was now home. Granted, it didn't feel like it yet, but she was sure it would eventually. It just took time. And it wasn't as if she was locked in a cave somewhere. She was free to leave, even be gone overnight. But just for one night at a time, she reminded herself. And that was okay. She'd take day trips, explore Colorado, e-mail her sisters and friends and keep in touch with what was going on in London. And since Spencer had betrayed her, she'd been rethinking her plan to open a dress shop with Priscilla in London after she finished her internship. Maybe Colorado would be better. She'd check out possible shop locations. So she had plenty to do. She'd be fine.

So why did she feel like crying?

"Are you all right?"

Startled, Elizabeth whirled to find John Cassidy studying her with dark-brown eyes that saw far more than she liked. Irritated, she scowled at him. "Don't do that!"

For just a moment, she thought she saw the glint of amusement in his eyes, but he blinked and it was gone. "I beg your pardon," he said stiffly. "Don't do what?"

"Sneak up on me! You scared me."

"That wasn't my intention," he retorted, "but you need to be scared. Being on guard is probably the only thing that's going to save that pretty little ass of yours."

"Excuse me?"

His lips twitched, and this time, he made no effort to hide the wicked humor that flashed in his eyes. "There's no need for that. I'm just trying to keep you safe. If something happens to you, I've got to call Buck, and then there's going to be hell to pay."

She lifted a delicately arched brow at him. "Oh, really? So what are you saying? He'd blame you or me?"

"I'd just as soon not take a chance," he said smoothly. "Behave yourself, watch your back, and we'll both get along fine."

"Behave myself!" she sputtered, indignantly. "Do you know who you're talking to?"

Not the least intimidated by her, he grinned. "Elizabeth Wyatt, oldest sister, the responsible one. I can think of other ways to describe you, but I think I'd better stop there."

She was so irritated, steam was practically coming out of her ears. She didn't, however, blast him as she so obviously wanted to. Instead, she said through clenched teeth, "We need to get something straight, Mr. Cassidy, before we go any further. I'm your boss. You don't tell me to behave myself or how to get along with you. *You* have to worry about how to get along with *me.* Understood?"

He should have said, "Yes, ma'am," and apologized for so obviously insulting her. It would have been the wise thing to do since she did, probably, have the power to fire his ass. But pushing Miss Elizabeth Wyatt's buttons, he was discovering, was too damn easy. There were just some things a man couldn't resist.

"You're my boss?" he repeated, making no effort to hide his mocking grin. "Yeah, right."

"You don't believe me? Well, how about this, Mr. Cassidy? You're fired!"

Far from impressed, he only laughed. "Sorry, sweetheart. I work for Buck. You don't have the power to fire me."

Chapter 2

Outraged, Elizabeth couldn't believe his audacity. So she didn't have the power to fire him, did she? Well, they'd see about that! He worked for the Wyatts—all four Wyatts—and if he had trouble accepting that, then she'd call Buck and *he* would make him understand who was in charge of the Broken Arrow for the next month. And if he still refused to accept who his bosses were, then Mr. Cassidy could find himself somewhere else to work. It was that simple.

But even as she considered going into the house to call Buck, she realized what she was doing and stiffened. No, she thought, irritated. She didn't need Buck to back her up—this was her ranch, too, and she was in charge! If John didn't like it, then too damn bad!

"Don't push me, Mr. Cassidy." she warned. "If you don't realize that you'll be the one who loses, then you're not as smart as I think you are."

For a moment she thought he was going to ignore her advice completely, but something in her tone must have told him she was serious. With a mocking curl of his mouth, he nodded his head slightly and lifted a finger to the brim of his black Stetson. "Yes, ma'am. Whatever you say, ma'am. Now, if you'll excuse me, I have work to do."

He strode past her and headed for the barn. He didn't once look back, and that was probably a good thing. Because she couldn't take her eyes off his lean backside. The man had no right to look so good in a denim work shirt and worn jeans. Were his jeans as soft as they looked? His body as hard? With no trouble whatsoever, she could see him working in the sun, his shirt hung on a fence post, his sweat-damp muscles rippling as he worked—

Elizabeth Marie Wyatt! What has gotten into you?

Shocked by her own thoughts, she stiffened. What was she doing? She didn't fantasize about men she didn't know. Especially a man like John Cassidy. All right, so he was an incredibly handsome man in a hard, macho way. He was also far too sure of himself, not to mention opinionated and argumentative and an employee. Any woman who made the mistake of getting involved with him would find herself with her hands full.

She wasn't that foolish, Elizabeth assured herself. She liked a man who was more sophisticated, less rugged, softer. She doubted John Cassidy had ever been soft a day in his life, including the day he was born.

Still, she couldn't stop thinking about that rock-hard body of his. What would it feel like to be held against that body? To have him move over her, in her—

Suddenly realizing the turn her thoughts had made, she pulled herself up short, horrified. What was wrong with her? She wasn't the type of woman who mooned over a man she didn't know, let alone fantasized about having sex with him! Did John know? If he even suspected what was going on in her head, she'd be completely mortified.

This was all Spencer's fault, she decided. She was still hurt, still reeling from his betrayal and obviously looking for a distraction. It wasn't going to be John Cassidy!

Work, she thought desperately, turning to stride into the house. She needed to focus on what was really important—deciding what she was going to do with her future, where she was going to live, work.

Nothing else mattered but that. Certainly not a man, not romance, not love.

Clinging to that thought, she stepped into Buck's office and settled at the computer. Within minutes she was on the Internet, checking out Colorado towns and cities, searching for just the right location for an eclectic dress shop. And whenever she found her thoughts drifting to the ranch and the man she was sharing it with, she determinedly brought her attention back to the matter at hand.

The afternoon flew by, and without quite knowing how it happened, she heard the grandfather clock in the hall strike five. Pleased, she hurriedly printed out the info she'd spent the day collecting so that she could study it later, then headed for the kitchen. She hadn't had anything to eat since breakfast, and she was starving.

The refrigerator was overflowing with the barbecue leftover from the reception, and she would have sworn the only thought in her head was eating. Then she heard John's truck in the back drive. In the time it took to draw in a quick breath, she realized that she'd been listening for him all afternoon. Before she could stop herself, she stepped over to the window that sat above the kitchen's deep, old-fashioned cast-iron sinks and looked out.

Although she didn't move, didn't wave, didn't do

anything to draw attention to herself as he pulled up next to the barn and parked, somehow he must have sensed he was being watched. He glanced toward the house suddenly, and in the gathering twilight, their eyes locked.

Time jarred to a sudden stop. How long they stood there, staring at each other across the homestead compound, she couldn't have said. Then he nodded mockingly and strode over to the small cabin where he lived at the edge of the compound. It wasn't until he disappeared inside that Elizabeth realized he'd stolen the air right out of her lungs.

How, she wondered shakily, was she supposed to ignore a man who could do that to her without coming anywhere near her?

That was a question that plagued her the rest of the evening. Regardless of how hard she tried to dismiss him from her thoughts, knowing that he was now just across the compound, within calling distance, changed everything. She decided to have just a salad for dinner and found herself wondering what he was having. Did he watch television in the evenings? Or work? When did he take a shower—

Frustrated and thoroughly disgusted with herself, she ate only half her salad, then spent the next two hours going over the info she'd collected on the Internet. When she finally went to bed at ten, she was exhausted. She still hadn't adjusted to the time change and could hardly keep her eyes open.

Her night, however, was far from restful. She dreamed of Buck and Rainey and the love everyone at the wedding could feel…John and the challenge in his eyes when he told her she wasn't his boss…a faceless enemy hiding in the shadows, waiting to reach out and grab her, hurt her—

Coming awake abruptly, her heart slamming against her ribs, she glanced at the clock on the nightstand and groaned in the darkness. Four o'clock. She had to turn her brain off! But when she punched her pillow into a more comfortable position and drifted back to sleep, the images that filled her dreams tugged her back to wakefulness again and again. By the time the sun peeked over the eastern horizon, she was exhausted. With a groan, she gave up and rolled out of bed.

Two hours later, after a shower and a pot of tea, her eyes were finally open. After all the research she'd done last night, she'd planned to check out locations for her shop, but she hesitated at the thought of driving. She could use the ranch pickup, but she hadn't even tried driving in America yet, and today wasn't a good day to start. She was tired and far from alert, and just the thought of getting behind the wheel and driving on the wrong side of the road set her heart pounding. She'd go another day, she assured herself. Today, she'd stick around the house and take it easy.

But doing nothing all day just wasn't in her DNA. By ten o'clock in the morning, the silence of the house was closing in on her and she was going crazy. In desperation, she stepped outside and found herself wishing for the garden she had back home.

So plant one, a voice in her head retorted. *There's a perfect spot for a rose garden right outside the breakfast room. You can enjoy it every morning while you're having breakfast.*

Delighted with the idea, she inspected the area and decided that it would work nicely. She would ask John to clear away the grass, then drive her into town for the rosebushes she would need. With the right tools, she could plant them herself.

Pleased that she'd come up with a way to leave her mark on the ranch, she went looking for John and found him in the barn, cleaning out the hayloft. In the dusty, late-morning light, the man looked as if he belonged on a calendar. She took one look at him and wanted to touch.

Heat climbing into her cheeks, she felt at a distinct disadvantage as she frowned up at him. "Can you stop for a moment? I need to talk to you."

Stepping over to the edge of the loft, he lifted a dark brow at her. "So talk."

Her eyes narrowed dangerously. "If you're going to work here, Mr. Cassidy, I would appreciate some measure of respect."

Not the least impressed with the threat, he only grinned. "Yes, ma'am. Anything you say, ma'am. Is there anything else, ma'am?"

"Yes," she snapped, her blue eyes shooting daggers at him. "I need the small plot of land by the breakfast room cleared so I can plant a rose garden. Then you can drive me into town so I can buy the roses."

"No problem. How does Friday morning sound?"

"Friday!"

"I'm busy," he retorted. "I've got some time Friday morning."

If looks could kill, he would have dropped dead right there on the spot. "There seems to be a misunderstanding. I'm not waiting until Friday. I want to get this done today."

Even as the words were coming out of her mouth, she realized that she sounded like a spoiled brat. Mortified, she wanted to kick herself, but there was something about John, about the way he looked at her, *challenged* her, that rubbed her the wrong way. And he knew it. She could see the glint in his eye. He knew how to push her buttons with nothing more than a quirk of his brow, and he loved it!

Not the least impressed with the fact that she was

pulling rank, he just looked at her. "Sorry, sweetheart, but if you want a rose garden put in today, then you're doing it yourself. I'm not a gardener, I'm a foreman in charge of a one-man operation while your brother's gone, and I've got work to do."

"Yes, you do," she retorted, cringing at her inability to shut her mouth. "You have some ground to clear for my garden."

"Fat chance," he replied, sobering. "And before you remind me that you're my boss, let me tell you a thing or two, Miss High and Mighty. When you know something about ranching and what it takes to run a ranch, we'll talk about whether you're my boss or not. You don't know how to ride a horse, rope, repair a fence. Hell, I bet you can't even collect eggs from the chicken coop, let alone make homemade biscuits. If you're going to be a woman rancher, you need to at least know how to feed your ranch hands."

Indignant, she snapped, "I'll have you know, I *can* make biscuits! And as for collecting eggs, any six-year-old can do that."

"Really? Then why haven't you? The chicken coop's on the south side of the barn...or hadn't you noticed?"

Not missing the challenging glint in his eyes, she should have told him to go kiss a duck; she didn't have to prove herself to him. But she was afraid he would accuse her of being afraid, and he would have been right. Ever since she was a little girl, she'd been afraid of chickens and horses, and she didn't even know why. She just knew she wanted no part of either.

Her pride, however, wouldn't let her admit that. Chiding herself for being so easily manipulated, she turned on her heel and headed for the chicken coop. And with every step she took, the fear that was lodged deep in her throat grew thicker and thicker.

Behind her, she never saw John scramble down the hayloft ladder…or the grin of admiration that tugged at his mouth as he followed her. Two steps behind her, his gaze trained on her slim back, he had to admit that the lady had a way about her.

He'd never seen a woman less eager to deal with a chicken. The second she reached the door to the chicken coop, she stopped dead in her tracks. Fighting a grin, he said innocently, "Problem?"

"No!"

"Then let me get the door for you."

He stepped around her and pulled open the small door to the chicken coop. Grinning, he motioned for her to precede him. "Ladies first."

Another woman would have told him to go to hell. Instead she said, "Stuff it," and stepped through the door.

That was as far as she got. Her gaze settled on the

ten hens sitting on their nests, staring at her with wary eyes, and she couldn't go any farther. John found himself sympathizing. The first time he'd had to gather eggs, he'd been more than a little terrified, himself. Of course, he'd hadn't even been in school yet. Elizabeth was a long way from that.

"Don't let them scare you," he said quietly. "Give me your hand."

She looked at him like he'd lost his mind. "Do I look like a fool?"

"Far from it," he chuckled. "Give me your hand, Elizabeth." When she hesitated, he rolled his eyes. "I'm not going to let anything hurt you. C'mon, just give me your hand."

Even as he said the words, he realized that she really had no reason to trust him. She barely knew him, and the fact that he was the Broken Arrow's ranch foreman meant nothing. The last foreman not only blew up the ranch's old Spanish mine, which had been lost for two hundred years before Buck and Rainey found it again, but he'd also tried to kill Rainey. John couldn't blame Elizabeth for not trusting anyone in Colorado except her family. He'd have felt the same way if he'd been in her shoes.

"I'm just going to show you how to handle the chickens," he said quietly. "We may butt heads, and I may tease the hell out of you, but I don't get my kicks hurting women. So if that's what you're afraid of—"

"No!" she said too quickly, color stinging her cheeks. "I know that.... I didn't mean to imply—"

"Then give me your hand. If you're going to be the boss..."

He had her there and they both knew it. She glared at him, and he just barely suppressed a smile when she stepped forward and slapped her hand into his. Then his fingers closed around hers.

Whatever he'd been expecting, it wasn't the heat that jumped from her hand to his. Frowning, he stared down at their joined hands. Why hadn't he noticed how small and delicate her hands were? And her skin...could he ever in a million years have guessed how soft it was?

"I realize you've probably never held a woman's hand before," she said dryly, "but you can't keep mine. I'm sort of attached to it."

Suddenly jerked back to his surrounding, he glanced up abruptly and found her watching him with a wry glint in her blue eyes. Caught red-handed, he was shocked to feel himself blush. "I can see why you would be," he quipped, releasing her. "It's a nice hand. Soft. Not used to a lot of work."

"There you go again," she sighed. "Just when I thought I could like you—"

"I opened my mouth and ruined it," he chuckled. "Don't worry, we're about to toughen you up. First, we'll start with the chickens and then move on to riding and roping and riding fence. So go ahead…get an egg."

Elizabeth couldn't believe he was serious. "And how would you suggest I do that?"

"By putting your hand under the hen," he said patiently. "Just reach under her and grab an egg."

He made it sound so simple. If she hadn't dreaded the thought of acting like even more of a coward in front of him, she would have put her hand behind her back like a scared little girl. Instead she lifted her chin and stepped forward with the confidence of a woman who'd been collecting eggs all her life. The hen took one look at her and decided she meant business. She didn't so much as ruffle a feather as Elizabeth stole an egg from her.

It wasn't until she saw the egg in her hand that Elizabeth realized what she'd done. Shocked, she laughed, "Oh, my God! I did it!"

Delighted with herself, she was practically glowing, and John couldn't take his eyes off her. He tried to convince himself that she was a snotty, snippy Englishwoman who was far too bossy for his taste, but he had to admit that she had guts. She clearly had a fear of chickens, but not only had she not admitted that, but she'd accepted his dare in spite of it. How could he dislike a woman like that? Especially when she was so damn beautiful? When she laughed, her whole face lit up. And he'd never been able to resist a woman who liked to laugh.

You'd better start resisting her, the voice of reason drawled in his head. *She's the boss's sister. How do you think Buck would feel if he knew you had the hots for his sister?*

He didn't have an answer for that, didn't even want to go there. He needed his job and he wasn't risking it for Elizabeth Wyatt or any other woman. All he wanted to do was work and get on with his life. That wasn't a hell of a lot to ask.

Then why, he wondered, did he have such a difficult time remembering the woman was off-limits? Okay, so she was beautiful. Her skin was like cream, and when she smiled, he felt the punch of it right in his gut. But he wasn't looking for a woman, and even if he had been, she was the last woman on earth he would have chosen. Not only did she have the power to sign his paycheck, she also had no intention of living in Colorado, or the United States, for that matter. As soon as Buck returned from his honeymoon, she'd return to England. That's where her life was...and, no doubt, the man she was currently involved with.

And there was a man, he thought grimly. There

had to be—a woman with her looks and class didn't go through life alone. Not unless the men in England were idiots, and he didn't think that was the case.

So why are you standing here, staring at her like she just stepped out of some crazy fantasy? Get the hell out of here and get back to work!

Blinking as if he'd just stepped out of a fog, he took a quick step back. "That's all there is to it," he said coolly. "Grab one of the buckets by the door and just start collecting eggs."

"Then what?"

"Take them to the house and rinse them off, then dry them and store them in the refrigerator. If you have any problems, I'll be in the shop working on the tractor. I've got to start planting by the end of the week—"

"Planting? You farm?"

He nodded. "We plant alfalfa in the lower pastures below the tree line. And if I don't get it in soon, the crop will come in late and we'll be lucky if we cut the fields before the first snowfall. I'd better get back to the tractor. Call if you need help."

He strode out with nothing more than a wave, leaving Elizabeth with the chickens. Given her druthers, she would have turned and followed John out, but she knew he was right. This was as much her ranch as it was her brother and sisters' and she needed to know how every phase of the place operated. Her heart thumping, her jaw set at a determined angle, she approached the next chicken with a glint in her eye that warned her she was going to be Sunday dinner if she so much as squawked. She didn't.

When she didn't see John for the rest of the afternoon, Elizabeth told herself it was probably for the best. He was an employee, and he was the type of man who wouldn't ever let her forget that. Not that she wanted to, she reminded herself grimly. Spencer's betrayal was still fresh in her mind and heart and probably would be for a long time.

The quickest way to get over one man is to find another.

She winced at the old adage. No. No. No! She wasn't going there, wasn't even going to consider it. If she knew nothing else about John Cassidy, she knew he wasn't the kind of man a woman walked away from easily. Buck and Rainey would be back from their honeymoon in a month, and she didn't know where she would be after that. Colorado? London? Maybe even California or New York. It all depended on where she decided to open her shop. Wherever it was, she wasn't leaving her heart behind.

The matter settled, she spent the rest of the day in Buck's office, acquainting herself with what it took to run the business end of the ranch, and she didn't once look out the window for John. She thought she heard the tractor several times, but she determinedly pulled her attention back to the ranch's financial statements.

By the time she shut the computer down, it was going on nine in the evening. After sitting at a desk for so many hours, she was stiff and sore and in desperate need of a long soak in the tub. When she stepped into her bedroom to collect her nightgown and robe, however, the thought of a bath flew right out of her head when she spied the note lying on her pillow.

A frown etched her brow. What the dickens was John up to? It had to be from him, of course—they were the only two people on the ranch. But why would he leave a note on her pillow? Or, for that matter, come into her bedroom? If he had something to say to her, all he had to do was knock on the office door—she'd been working at Buck's desk all day.

Her heart in her throat, she stepped over to the bed and without touching it, studied the single piece of paper that had been folded in half. On the outside, her name was sloppily written in a script she didn't recognize. She hadn't seen John's handwriting, but she would have thought that his would be neater.

Don't touch it, a voice in her head warned. *Go find him and see if he wrote the note.*

Hesitating, she considered that option, but what if

it really was from him? Then she'd feel like an idiot. Making a snap decision, she picked up the piece of paper and pulled it open.

LEAVE WHILE YOU STILL CAN!

Her blood suddenly pounding in her ears, she dropped the note lightning quick. John was responsible for this, she told herself, and desperately tried to believe it. He had access to the house and motive he didn't like answering to her. He probably thought that if he could convince her to leave, Buck would come back early from his honeymoon and he wouldn't have to deal with her anymore.

As far as theories went, Elizabeth knew it was half-baked. But she wouldn't allow herself to consider anything else when she was completely alone in the house and so scared she could taste it. Picking up the note by the corner with fingers that were far from steady, she hurried downstairs and outside to John's cabin.

"I want to know what the meaning of this is right now!" she bellowed the second he opened the door to her. "If you think you can scare me into leaving, then you've wasted your time."

Surprised, he scowled. "What the devil are you talking about?"

"This!" she snapped, and waved a piece of paper in his face.

Without a word, he snatched it out of her hand and read it, only to glance up at her sharply. "Where'd you get this?"

"On my pillow," she replied. "And don't pretend you don't know anything about it. You had to do it. You're the only one here."

If she thought he would deny it, she was doomed to disappointment. Instead, he walked straight to the phone on the table next to the couch and dialed 911. "I need the sheriff," he told the dispatcher curtly. "There's been a break-in at the Broken Arrow Ranch."

"Is the intruder still in the house?"

"Not that I know of," he retorted, "but I can't be sure of that. I don't even know how he got in."

"Is anyone hurt? Do you need an ambulance?"

"No...just the sheriff and a couple of his men to search the place. I could do it, but—"

"No!" the dispatcher said quickly. "Please don't take that chance. There's a deputy on the way—he should be there shortly. In the meantime, do you have any weapons?"

"I've got a shotgun and I'm not afraid to use it," he retorted. "Right now, Ms. Wyatt and I are in the foreman's cabin behind the barn. If anyone touches my front door, I'm shooting first and asking questions later, so make sure the deputy knows to come in with sirens blazing."

"I'll pass that message along," she assured him. "Someone should be there any second."

The words were hardly out of her mouth when the sound of sirens cut sharply through the night air. Glancing out the window near the front door, John watched as a county patrol car skidded to a stop in a cloud of dust before his cabin. He didn't unlock the door, however, until he saw who stepped out of the car.

"Looks like we got the top dog," John told Elizabeth. "The sheriff himself. Not," he added, "that that means a hell of a lot. From what Buck told me, law enforcement around here's nothing but a joke. I guess we're about to find out."

He opened the door at the sheriff's sharp knock and held out his hand to him in greeting. "Glad you could get here so quickly, Sheriff. I'm John Cassidy. And this is Elizabeth Wyatt."

"Glad to meet you," the other man said amiably, shaking his hand, then stepping over to Elizabeth to do the same. "I'm Sherm Clark, Ms. Wyatt. What's this about an intruder?"

"I found a note in my bedroom warning me to leave while I still could," she said grimly, nodding to the single piece of paper John had laid on the lamp table by the front window. "Since John and I are the only ones on the ranch, someone else was obviously here."

"Did you see anyone else?" he asked as he stepped over to the table and carefully picked up the paper with a pair of tweezers. "Hear anything?"

"Nothing," she retorted. "I've been working in the ranch office all day. I saw the note when I went up to my room to collect some things for a bath. The note was on my pillow."

"And where were you?" he asked John.

"Here in my cabin. I worked on the tractor all day and had just finished taking a shower myself when Elizabeth showed up at my door with the note."

"So neither one of you saw anyone." Frowning, he slipped the note into an evidence bag, then glanced up sharply at John. "Did you touch the note?"

He nodded. "But just on the right hand corner. Both of our prints are on there."

"Then I'll need you both to come down to the office tomorrow and have your fingerprints taken. Then we'll send the note to the state lab and see who else has been handling this."

Studying him shrewdly, John said, "You don't really expect any other prints to be on there, do you?"

He shrugged. "I don't have any expectations one way or the other. I'm just doing my job and following up on the evidence. Speaking of which, I need to dust the doors and Ms. Wyatt's bedroom for prints. The exterior doors to the house were locked, weren't they?"

When both men looked at her, Elizabeth wanted to sink right through the floor. "Not yet," she admitted huskily. "I usually lock them right before I go upstairs at night, but I was distracted and completely forgot about it."

"Elizabeth! You know what's been going on around here—"

"I know. I wasn't thinking. It was stupid—"

"You were lucky this time," the sheriff told her. "This is a big house. If someone wanted to harm you, they could slip in through an unlocked door, hide out until nightfall, then slit your throat while you're sleeping. Keep your doors locked at all times."

Blanching, she pressed a hand to her throat. "I will," she said huskily.

"You don't have to scare her to death," John said, scowling.

"She needs to know what can happen," the older man said flatly. "Don't underestimate people, especially someone who wants what you have."

"Trust me, I won't," Elizabeth said. "I'm going to keep everything locked. I'll carry my keys with me everywhere I go in the house and on the property, even if it's just outside to the chicken coop to collect the eggs. I'm not going through this again."

"Good," Sherm Clark retorted. "Now show me your bedroom."

Chapter 3

There was no sign of a break-in. The front and back doors, as well as the door to Elizabeth's room, were dusted for prints, but the sheriff made no secret of the fact that the only fingerprints he expected to find were those of John and Elizabeth.

"Not," he quickly pointed out, "that I think either of one of you are lying about who wrote the note or how it ended up on Elizabeth's pillow. All I know is that someone put it there. Give me a logical explanation of who that someone was and I'll be happy to check it out."

Frustrated, Elizabeth wasn't the least bit fooled. She

didn't care what he said, he obviously thought either she or John was responsible for the note. He refused to even consider any other possibility. Irritating man! What kind of sheriff was he? If John had written the note as some kind of twisted joke, he wouldn't have insisted on calling the authorities. So that left her. Why would she write a note to herself, then let John call the sheriff? What purpose would it serve?

"I'm sleeping on the couch," John told her bluntly after the sheriff left.

Her heart skipped a beat at the thought. "That's not necessary. As long as the doors are locked—"

"I'm not taking any chances with your safety," he said flatly. "If you don't like it, call Buck."

She wasn't going to do that, and they both knew it. "Fine," she retorted. "Have it your way. I'm going to bed. You don't have to sleep on the couch—there's a downstairs guest room."

"The couch in the family room is better—it's close to the stairs. I'll be able to hear you if you need help."

She wasn't going to need help—she had to believe that or she wouldn't sleep a wink. But all she said was, "Fine. If that's the way you want it." Retrieving a blanket and pillow from the downstairs linen closet for him, she said, "I guess I'll see you in the morning. Good night."

She felt his eyes on her all the way up the stairs,

and it was all she could do not to look back. What was it about the man that made it impossible for her to ignore him? she wondered as she reached her room and began to get ready for bed. She was upstairs, he was down, and she knew it was impossible to hear what he was doing. Still, she could have sworn that she could hear every breath he took. She had to be losing her mind.

Irritated with herself for being so fanciful, she crawled into bed a few moments later and closed her eyes with a tired sigh. She might as well have tried to catch forty winks in the middle of the Denver airport—it wasn't going to happen. Frustrated, she punched her pillow into a more comfortable position, but even though she felt safe with John sleeping downstairs, she couldn't put the note out of her head. She might not know the name of whoever left the warning on her pillow, but it was obviously someone who thought they had a chance of inheriting the ranch by scaring her into leaving.

It wasn't going to happen, she vowed grimly. She wasn't going to be the one who let the family down. And she wasn't going to live in fear or hide in her room on her own ranch!

The decision made, she finally fell asleep and was up the next morning with the sun. If she expected to catch John still sleeping, she was doomed to disappointment. Not only was he already awake, but he'd returned the pillow and blanket he'd used to the linen closet, started a pot of coffee in the kitchen, then locked the back door on his way out.

He was, she had to admit, thoughtful. But she needed a heck of a lot more from him than thoughtfulness. Grabbing a cup of coffee, she went in search of him and found him in the barn loading fencing supplies into the back of the ranch pickup.

He looked up in surprise at her entrance, but before he could say a word of greeting, she said, "I thought you already repaired the fence."

"The ranch is fifty square miles," he retorted. "Repairing fences is a never ending process." Throwing the last roll of barbwire into the bed of the truck, he studied her with a sudden frown. "What are you doing up so early? You haven't found any more notes, have you?"

"What? Oh, no, thank God! I just couldn't sleep. I'm just so angry!"

"I don't blame you," he told her. "Whoever left that note is nothing but a coward."

"He's wasting his time," she said flatly. "I'm not going anywhere and neither is my family. This is our ranch, and no one's taking it from us. If that means it comes down to a fight, then so be it."

John had seen her frustrated before, but he'd never

seen her so stirred up. She was furious, and she had every right to be. She and Buck and her sisters weren't doing anything except trying to live up to the terms of Hilda Wyatt's will. And because of that, they were getting harassed by some thugs who didn't think they were entitled to the place. Too damn bad! The Wyatts were Hilda's legitimate heirs and the will was valid. They were staying.

"I told Buck when he hired me that he could count on me to help any way I could," he told her quietly. "That promise extends to you and your sisters. Anyone who even thinks about going after you is going to have to go through me first. You know that, don't you?"

Surprise flared in her eyes. "I appreciate that," she said huskily. "Thank you."

"You're not in this alone. If there's anything I can do..."

"You can help me make this ranch mine," she said simply. "I thought about it last night, and I'm not going to cower in my room like some scaredy-cat who jumps at her own shadow. I'm not going to live in fear. This is the Wyatt family homestead and I'm a Wyatt. I'm going to work this ranch like I own it."

A slight smile curled the corners of his mouth. "You *do* own it. So I guess this means you want to know how to do something more than gather eggs."

"I do. You were right. If I'm going to be the boss,

I need to know everything that's involved in running the ranch. I need you to teach me."

"Then let's go ride fence," he said promptly, then caught her off guard when he tossed her the keys. "You drive."

"What? Me? Are you joking? I can't drive. I'm not used to driving on the right side of the road."

Amused, he only grinned. "There aren't any roads where we're going, so it doesn't matter. Just don't hit a tree or knock the fence down and we'll get along fine."

Her heart pounding, Elizabeth was in no mood to appreciate his sense of humor. Did he know what he was asking of her? It wasn't only driving on the opposite side of the road that was the problem, it was the steering wheel and the pedals and everything else being opposite of where they were supposed to be. She wasn't ready!

John, however, didn't give her a chance to voice a second objection. Walking around the truck, he slid into the passenger seat. "Oh, yeah," he asked innocently as he watched her gingerly settle behind the steering wheel, "you do know how to drive a standard, don't you?"

In the process of slipping the key into the ignition, she looked sharply at the long gearshift that stuck out of the floorboard in front of the old pickup's bench seat. "Oh, God."

John's lips twitched. "Why do I have the feeling this could be a problem?"

"Because it is," she retorted, horrified. "I don't even know where to start."

"First," he chuckled. "You always start in first."

When she just looked at him, he almost laughed. Did she have any idea how funny she was? He almost asked her, but he had a feeling she wouldn't appreciate the question in her current mood. "Well?" he asked, lifting a dark brow at her when she just sat there. "What are you waiting for?"

"You to show me where first is," she replied. "How am I supposed to find it when it's not marked?"

"Push the clutch in," he said, nodding toward the pedal next to the brake. "That's it. Now put it in first." When she just looked at him, he reached across the distance between them and brought her hand to the stick shift. A split second later, his fingers closed over hers and he moved the gearshift into first.

Unable to take her eyes off his hand covering hers, Elizabeth told herself she was just trying to figure out where the different gears were, but she knew it was more than that. She barely knew him. How could his touch feel so right?

"When you shift into second, you have to hang your head out the window and howl at the moon."

Caught up in her thoughts, his words suddenly

registered. Frowning in confusion, she looked up at him in surprise. "What?"

"Just seeing if you're listening," he said dryly. "I thought I lost you there for a minute."

Hot color singeing her cheeks, she dropped her gaze back to their joined hands. "I was just—"

...wondering what your hands would feel like moving all over my body.

The thought shook her to the core...and heated her blood. Mortified, she didn't dare meet his gaze. Did he realize what he was doing to her? What she was thinking? She had to stop this! Before he guessed—

"Why do I have the feeling that I've lost you again?" he asked, amused. "Was it something I said? If you don't want to do this—"

"No!" she said quickly, jerking herself back to attention. "I was just trying to figure out where second is."

"It's a standard H," he told her. "Keep the clutch in and bring the gearshift straight back. That's it. Now shift over to third— Good girl! And down to fourth. That's it."

"That's all? Why, that shouldn't be difficult at all!"

He grinned. "Once you get the hang of it, you can do it in your sleep and not even think about it. The hard part is giving it gas and letting the clutch out without killing it. That takes some practice. So ease up on the clutch as you give it some gas. Easy. Easy. Not so fast! You—"

"Killed it," she finished for him. "Darn! We didn't even move!"

"You'll get it," he chuckled. "It just takes practice. Try letting the clutch out slower."

She tried. And tried. Then, with no warning, the wheels began to turn. "Oh, my God! We're moving!"

"You're damn straight we're moving!" he laughed. "Now shift into second. That's it. Easy," he growled, wincing as the gears ground in protest. "Ease up on the clutch—"

With a jerk, the truck died again.

Elizabeth, however, was far from discouraged. Grinning, she reached for the key and started the truck again. "I can do this," she said, grinning like a kid with a new toy. "I've just got to get the footwork down."

"And watch where you're going," he advised as she picked up a little speed and headed west, away from the house. "Watch that tree!"

"I see it...I think." Laughing, she swerved around it, and shifted into third.

Just that easily, she conquered shifting and no longer needed John's guidance on the gearshift. Torn between relief and disappointment that he no longer had a reason to touch her, he released her and told himself it was for the best. Her skin was too soft, her smile too intoxicating. Thrilled with herself, she acted as if he'd just handed her the moon, and all he could think about was kissing her.

And it was all her fault, he thought with a frown. It was that scent she wore...it was guaranteed to drive a man crazy. And then there was the way her eyes lit up when she laughed. Did she have any idea how seductive she was? Or how much he wanted to touch her...kiss her?

Suddenly realizing where his thoughts had wandered, he stiffened and silently swore under his breath. What the hell was he doing?

"All right," Elizabeth said happily. "Where to?"

"Head over to the fence," he growled, nodding toward the barbwire fence fifty yards to the left, "and just keep driving the fence line. If you see a break, stop so I can fix it."

"No problem," she said, and shot across the pasture with a gurgle of laughter.

Minx, he thought, fighting a smile. Who would have thought the very proper Elizabeth would love driving across the pasture like a wild woman?

Practicing downshifting and shifting on the fly, Elizabeth couldn't remember the last time she had so much fun. More than once, John had to reach for the door frame to catch himself as she bounced over the rough terrain, and she caught a glimpse of his smile every time.

Then, just when she raced down a hill into a pasture that bordered a two-lane country road, she gasped at the sight of the cows that had escaped from the pasture and were walking down the road. "Oh, my God!"

Swearing, John immediately spied the break in the fence. "Dammit to hell! Pull over by that dead pine. It looks like the fence has been cut."

Cut didn't begin to describe it. Not only had someone cut all three strands of the barbwire that comprised the fence, but they'd also yanked two of the posts out of the ground and peeled the barbwire back. The cows didn't even hesitate as they streamed out of the pasture and sought greener grass along the sides of the road.

"What you want me to do?" Elizabeth asked as she quickly braked to a stop next to the cut fence and jumped out of the truck at the same time John did.

"Keep the cows from straying any farther down the road," he told her as he quickly grabbed his tools and supplies from the bed of the truck. "I'll need your help getting the cows back in, but for now, I've got to get the fence posts set in the ground and close the gap some."

Her heart jumping into her throat, Elizabeth looked at him like he'd lost his mind. "You want me to do *what?*"

If she expected him to be amused, she was in for a rude awakening. "This is no time to be a baby," he told her bluntly. "You're the owner, remember? If you don't get the cows off the road, and someone comes around the curve and plows into them, you're not only going to have a hell of a lawsuit on your hands, you may have someone's death on your conscience. Get to work!"

He didn't have to tell her twice, but as she hurried through the gap in the fence and found herself approaching twenty cows who were surveying her warily, her legs all but turned to jelly. He made it sound so simple. Just round them up and herd them back into the pasture. How? They outweighed her by four hundred pounds! And they had horns…sharp horns. If they turned on her—

"They're more scared of you than you are of them," he said, reading her mind as he knocked a new metal fence post into the ground. "Just get behind them and spread your arms wide as you start walking toward the break in the fence. And don't worry about getting them all in at once. Get a few in at a time, then go back for more."

Shaking in her shoes, she fought the need to run, and carefully made a wide circle around the cows until she was behind them. Most of them ignored her, but a few at the back of the herd glanced over their shoulders with narrow-eyed frowns full of distrust.

"Show 'em who's boss, Elizabeth. You're good at that."

From the corner of her eye, she could see John's wicked grin, but she didn't dare take her gaze off the cows. "Stuff it," she retorted. "You better be thinking what story you're going to tell my brother when I get killed in a stampede."

"A stampede," he laughed. "Sweetheart, I've worked with cows all my life and never seen a stampede. Trust me, that's not going to happen."

"Then why are they looking at me like they're going to flatten me?"

"You're just being paranoid. Act tough."

That was easy for him to say. She'd never been this close to a cow in her life! Frowning, she spread her arms wide and took a hesitant step forward. When the cows just looked at her, she rasped, "Move it, you big lugs, before you meet a car face-to-face and you end up becoming somebody's hamburger patty tonight!"

For a moment she didn't think they were going to budge. Then she took another hesitant step toward them, waiving her arms, and with more than one disrespectful flick of their tails, they turned and slowly moved toward the break in the fence.

"Yeah!" she laughed, exhilarated. "That's it. Move those tails. Oh, no!"

John didn't have to look to know what happened when the cows lifted their tails. Chuckling, he said, "Watch where you put your feet."

"Now you tell me!"

When she swore softly, he didn't dare look around. "You might want to clean your shoes before you get back in the truck," he said in a strangled voice. "In fact, you might want to throw them in the back when we leave."

"If I don't throw them at your head first," she said sweetly. "You're really enjoying this, aren't you?"

"No, of course not—"

Something hit him in the back. "I hope that's a clod of dirt," he told her as he began to unroll the barbwire. "I sure would hate to throw it back at you if it wasn't."

"Turn around and find out," she taunted. "I dare you."

He'd never been a man to walk away from a dare, and this time was no different. Glancing over his shoulder, he immediately spied a clod of dirt a few feet behind him on the ground. "Smart girl," he told her, making no attempt to hold back a grin. "I wasn't looking forward to making you ride in the back of the pickup with your shoes."

"It would never have happened," she retorted. "You're not my daddy. I don't have to obey you."

"You got that right," he agreed. "I'm not your daddy, thank God! And you may not have to obey me, but if I ever give you an order, you'd better damn sure do as I say because I wouldn't tell you to do something unless it was a matter of necessity."

"The boss doesn't take orders—"

"Everybody takes orders from somebody in their life," he tossed back, "regardless of— Watch out!"

Her eyes on him, Elizabeth didn't see the cow that suddenly noticed she'd been separated from her calf. One second the animal was meandering after her companions toward the break in the fence, and the next, she whirled, her eyes wide as she searched for her baby. And Elizabeth was right in her path.

Horrified, Elizabeth couldn't move, couldn't think, as her eyes locked with the cow's. Her mind screamed at her to run, but she stood frozen, her heart slamming against her ribs, unable to move so much as a single eyelash.

"Move!"

John's roar reached her as nothing else could. Startled, she blinked...just in time to see the cow bearing down on her with the fire of a protective mother gleaming in her eye. There was no time to think. Shrieking, she scrambled up a nearby boulder and just missed the brush of the cow's horns as she ran past.

Later, she couldn't have said how long she stood there, gasping, the thunder of her panic so loud in her ears that she couldn't hear John cussing like a sailor. In four long strides, he reached the pile of boulders she'd scrambled up on. "Are you all right? Did she get you with her horns?"

"No," she said shakily. "For a moment, though, I thought I was toast."

"Honey, the first thing you need to know about cattle is you *never* come between a mama and her baby. That's a good way to get trampled…or gored."

Still white as a sheet, she nodded. "Good point. I'll remember that."

"Let me help you down," he said huskily, holding a hand up to her. "You're safe now."

"Easy for you to say," she said, eyeing the cow that was now nuzzling its calf lovingly. "I don't trust her."

"Don't worry," he laughed. "I'll protect you from the big, bad cow. C'mon down from there. We've got a fence to fix."

"I'll fix the fence," she said as she placed her hand in his. "You deal with the cows."

Grinning, he closed his fingers around hers and held her steady as she started down the largest of the boulders. "You wanted to be boss," he reminded her. "That means—"

Her eyes on his, she didn't realize the curve of the

boulder was so steep until she found herself rushing down the rock. Before she could stop herself, her momentum carried her right into his arms.

"Oh, my God! I'm sorry—"

"Easy! Gotcha—"

In the time it took to blink, they were face-to-face and just inches apart, and John couldn't have said who was more startled. His eyes on the sweet, tempting curve of her mouth, he couldn't stop himself from pulling her closer. God, she felt good in his arms! It'd been a long time since he'd held a woman and forever since he'd kissed one. What would one kiss hurt? She wouldn't fire him…and if she did, it might damn sure be worth it!

He ignored the alarm bells clanging in his head and knew he could no more resist her than the cows could resist the lure of a downed fence. With a murmur that was her name, he covered her mouth with his.

Convinced he would never dare to kiss her, Elizabeth heard the voice in her head screaming at her to pull out of his arms and fire him on the spot. But how could she even think about firing the man when he kissed her with a hot need that turned her knees to butter? Did he know what he did to her? That no man had ever destroyed her so easily? That she wanted to pull him right down to the ground with her and forget everything but the heat of his mouth and the feel of his body, hot and hard, against hers?

Before she could even think about giving in to that need, however, the sudden blare of a horn jerked them both back to their surroundings. Startled, they sprang apart and turned just in time to see an old man in a pickup that was as old as he was ease around one of the cows that had once again managed to make its way through the downed fence.

Swearing, John stepped past her and hurried to herd the cows back onto Wyatt property and out of harm's way. Heat burning her cheeks, Elizabeth hurried after him. "Here...let me help."

His only response was a grunt of compliance, and within minutes, they had the rest of the cows on the correct side of the fence. Her heart still pounding, Elizabeth kept waiting for him to make some reference to the all-too-short kiss they'd shared, but the only conversation he directed her way was instructions on how to fix the fence. Had it meant nothing to him? she wondered. Or did he regret it and just didn't want to talk about it?

Hurt squeezed her heart at the thought, surprising her. It was just a kiss. Why was she getting all caught up in something that had hardly lasted a heartbeat?

"Elizabeth? Hello? Hey, where'd you go off to? I thought you wanted to know how to fix the fence?"

Jerked back to her surroundings, she looked up to find him watching her with steady brown eyes that saw far too much. Hot color singeing her cheeks, she was tempted to ask him why he'd kissed her then acted as if it had never happened, but if he regretted it, she suddenly realized she didn't want to know.

"I do," she said quickly. "I was just wondering who taught you how to do this. Was your father a rancher?"

His eyes returning to the barbwire he was working with, he said gruffly, "My parents had a ranch outside of Cheyenne, Wyoming. It wasn't half as big as the Broken Arrow, but it was a nice spread."

"Then you were probably riding and roping as soon as you were big enough to walk."

He smiled slightly. "Pretty much. I had my first pony when I was three."

"So how did you end up in Colorado? Buck said you were a Navy SEAL. I would have thought you would have gone back to Wyoming when you got out of the service."

John hesitated. He wasn't one to talk about his past—he'd only told Buck about what happened when he was in the Navy because he'd known he was going to do a background check. But to his surprise, he found himself telling Elizabeth, "I did go back to Wyoming. My parents died and left me the ranch."

Obviously confused, she frowned. "I don't understand. If you have a ranch of your own, then why are you working for us?"

Too late he realized he should have kept his mouth shut about his past. One question led to another and answers he didn't want to give. If he wasn't careful, he'd end up telling her everything, and his gut knotted at the thought. He didn't want to see her face when he told her he'd killed a man.

"I no longer own the ranch," he said flatly. "We're done here. Let's move on."

Picking up his tools and the roll of barbwire he'd brought to repair the fence, he turned and headed back to the pickup. Left with no choice but to follow, Elizabeth studied the rigid line of his back and recognized a No Trespassing sign when she saw one. A dozen questions sprang to mind, but she didn't push the issue. He was entitled to his secrets.

Still, she found herself intrigued. What was his story? Why did he no longer own the ranch he'd grown up on and that his parents had obviously wanted him to have? What wasn't he telling her?

Chapter 4

The question nagged her all night long, but that was the least of her worries when she met him at the barn the following morning for her second lesson on duties every rancher needed to know. Her heart pounding crazily, she eyed the horse John had saddled for her, with more than a few misgivings. What she knew about horses was limited to a single ride in the park with friends years ago. All she remembered about the event—besides her nervousness—was how sore she'd been the next day.

"I don't know about this," she told John, frowning

warily at the sorrel mare. "She seems awfully skittish. Maybe we should wait until she calms down."

"She is calm," he told her dryly. "You're the one who's skittish. You haven't ridden before, have you?"

Her chin came up at that. "Yes, I have."

"Oh, really? How many times?"

"Enough to know that I'm not good at it." When he just looked at her, waiting, she sighed, "Okay. Once. Is that what you wanted to hear?"

"It's for your safety," he pointed out, "not mine. I presume that was years ago?"

Lifting her pert nose in the air, she sniffed, "I was little more than a child."

"Ah, so just last year," he said with a slight smile. "So we'll start with basics. This is Rusty. She's a three-year-old and the best cutting horse we have."

Eyeing the mare critically, she frowned. "What do you mean...a cutting horse?"

"We use her to cut calves out of the herd so they can be inoculated and castrated." When her eyes widened, he chuckled. "That's life on a ranch, ma'am. And if you're going to be the boss..."

"I have to know how to do everything," she finished for him with a groan. "So where do we start?"

"With the horse," he said promptly, and patted the saddle. "This is a Western saddle, not an English one, so if you get in trouble, hang on to the pommel.

Be sure to keep your feet in the stirrups, and pull back on the reins to bring Rusty to a stop. She has a sensitive mouth, so you don't have to pull hard for her to get the message. You also use the reins to turn her in the direction you want her to go. Not," he added quickly, "that you need to do much once you pick out a calf. After that, all you have to do is sit there and look pretty and she'll do all the work."

Her heart skipped a beat at the left-handed compliment. He thought she was pretty? she thought, surprised. Or was he just teasing her?

"Any questions?"

She had a zillion questions. What were his secrets? Had he ever been in love? Surely he must have been. What happened to the woman he'd loved? Where was she? What—

"Was it something I said?" he teased. "I thought it was a simple question, but...maybe not."

A blush burned her cheeks. Outrageous man, she thought, fighting a smile. "I was just wondering where the ladder was."

Grinning, he brought a bucket over to the left side of the horse and turned it over so she could use it as a step. She lifted a delicately arched brow at him. "You can't be serious."

"C'mon, I'll help you," he chuckled. "Once you get your left foot in the stirrup, it's a piece of cake."

She could have pointed out that the horse was tall and she wasn't, but she refused to be a whiney baby. Reaching for the pommel to steady herself, she lifted her foot up to the stirrup and stepped into it.

Lifting herself up onto the back of the horse, however, was another matter. She considered herself in good shape, but she wasn't prepared for Rusty's height. She wavered slightly and was struggling to pull herself completely up onto the horse's back when she suddenly felt John's hand on her backside. Caught off guard, she gasped, and in the next instant, landed in the saddle.

Standing at her side, John looked up at her with an innocent look that didn't fool her for a minute. "I knew you could do it. Okay?"

"I would have made it on my own," she retorted, looking down her nose at him.

"Maybe," he agreed with a quick grin, "but it wouldn't have been nearly as much fun. So...are you ready?"

Her gaze turned to the cows and calves he'd herded into the coral. "I don't even know what I'm supposed to be doing," she admitted with a frown.

"That's okay," he assured her, patting her knee. "Rusty does. All you have to do is relax in the saddle and let her do the work." Handing her the reins, he nodded toward a cow with a twisted horn and her calf, which had wandered slightly away to investigate the hay that had been left for the cattle to eat. "There's a good one right there. Go for it."

Eyeing a cow from the back of a horse, Elizabeth discovered, was much less intimidating than from the ground. Encouraged, she tightened her fingers on the reins and with a gentle nudge of her heels and the click of her tongue, she sent the mare in the direction of the cow John had picked out. That was the last conscience decision she had to make. Rusty took off like a shot.

Startled, Elizabeth almost dropped the reins. If she hadn't grabbed the pommel, she would have slid right out of the saddle. "John!"

"Just relax," he called out to her, grinning. "You're doing great."

Relax? He couldn't be serious! How could she relax when Rusty was dodging and darting like a football player evading opposing team members on a mad dash to the goal? She couldn't anticipate the mare's next moves, what she was going to do next, what she was even trying to do…

"Her job is to separate the cow from her calf," John told her. "You have to move with her instead of against her. Relax your shoulders—stop holding your breath and just let go. There you go."

Following his instructions, Elizabeth would have

sworn that once she got off Rusty, she was never going to get on a horse again. Then she caught the mare's rhythm. Suddenly she found herself moving with the horse and laughed in surprise. "Oh, my God!"

"Way to go! I knew you could do it."

Dodging and darting with the mare, Elizabeth couldn't stop grinning. How could she not have seen the beauty of Rusty's motion? With a grace that was amazing for an animal its size, the horse moved like a dancer to a melody only she could hear, effortlessly separating the cow from her calf in a silent, beautiful ballet that Elizabeth loved.

"That was incredible!" she told John as he herded the calf into the chute where it would be inoculated and castrated. "How did you teach her to do that?"

"It's in the genes," he replied. "A good cutting horse is worth its weight in gold." Closing the gate on the chute, he turned to her with a grin. "Ready to go again?"

"Yes!"

"Go for it," he chuckled.

While she went to work isolating another calf, John took care of the calf in the chute. By the time he was finished, Elizabeth had separated another calf from its mother. He herded it into the chute, and the routine began all over again.

By the time all the calves were taken care of, it was the middle of the afternoon and Elizabeth felt as if she'd done a full days work. She was, however, thrilled. For the first time, she felt she belonged at the Broken Arrow Ranch. She still had a lot to learn, of course, but she was making progress.

"Good work," John told her with a grin as he moved to her side. "Your ancestors would be proud of you."

Surprised that he'd read her thoughts, she smiled, touched. "Thank you," she said huskily. "I like to think so."

"Here...let me help," he said, and lifted his hands to her waist as she swung her leg over the saddle and started to dismount.

Her heart tripping at his touch, Elizabeth reached blindly for the ground with her right foot. He was behind her, so close she only had to draw in a deep breath to feel his nearness. And for one timeless moment, when her feet finally settled on the ground, all she could think about was leaning back against him...just for a second.

But even as she toyed with the idea, she knew she couldn't give in to that particular temptation. Because if she did, she was afraid he would make her want something she couldn't have. Stiffening at the thought, she stepped away from him and started to turn, only to gasp in surprise as muscles that weren't used to riding tightened in protest. "Oh!"

"What? Are you all right? What's wrong?"

"My legs!" she gasped.

Frowning, he swept her off her feet before she could guess his intentions and quickly carried her to the pickup, where he carefully set her down on the truck's tailgate. "It's probably just cramps," he assured her. "It's been years since you've ridden."

When he pushed up the left pant leg of her jeans and began to massage the calf of her leg, she sucked in a sharp breath. "What are you doing?"

"Working out the stiffness," he retorted. "You need to soak in the hot tub tonight. Otherwise, you're not going to be able to walk tomorrow."

Her heart thundering, she just barely swallowed a groan. If she wasn't able to walk tomorrow, it would be because he melted every muscle in her body with just his touch. "I…I'm f-fine," she stuttered huskily, grabbing his hands before he could destroy her further. "I wasn't expecting my legs to be so shaky. They're better, thank you."

"No problem," he said easily. "You did a good job today. Thanks for your help."

"Thank you for teaching me," she replied.

"My pleasure."

Silence stretched between them, threatening to turn awkward. Heat climbing in her cheeks, she forced a weak smile. "I should go clean up, then soak in the hot tub. I'll see you later."

She told herself she didn't run into the house, but that was exactly what she did. She couldn't help it. If she didn't put some space between them, she knew she was going to ask him to join her in the hot tub, and that could be nothing but a mistake.

She had to get out of the house, she thought, shaken. She needed to mix with other people, strangers, anyone who would distract her from John and help her remember that she was returning to London in exactly three weeks, three hours and seventeen minutes. Why did she forget that every time she looked in John's eyes?

Hurrying upstairs, she decided to forego the hot tub for a shower instead, and quickly washed off the dirt of the day. She was still more than a little sore when she stepped out of the shower, but she didn't care. She was going into town for dinner.

Forty minutes later she stepped into the Rusty Bucket and seemed to draw the eye of every man in the place. Her brother had told her the steaks were terrific there, so she'd been expecting a steak house. Instead she discovered that the Rusty Bucket was a bar, and not a very sophisticated one. The tables were nothing more than rough-hewn picnic tables. Upside-down buckets wired with bare bulbs served as lighting, and the bar seemed to specialize in long-necks.

For all of five seconds she considered going to the twenty-four-hour diner down the street and just having pancakes for dinner. But she had her heart set on a steak. Refusing to even consider sitting at the bar, she turned away and found a small table for two in the far corner. Before she could even reach for the menu lodged between the salt and pepper shakers in the middle of the table, however, a cowboy broke away from the crowd at the bar.

"Hey, pretty lady. You look awfully lonely sitting there all by yourself. Why don't I join you and order both of us a steak?"

"Oh, I'm sorry," she said sweetly, "but I'm expecting someone. Maybe another time?"

Obviously not a man who was often turned down, he scowled. "Well, yeah, I guess."

Turning her attention to the menu, she didn't look up as the cowboy walked away in disappointment. Before she could even find the listing of entrees on the menu, another cowboy headed straight for her. She quickly dropped her eyes, hoping he would take the hint, but he wasn't so easily discouraged. He walked right up to her table and took a seat across from her without waiting for an invitation.

Glancing up, her eyes narrowed dangerously. "I'm expecting someone," she said coolly.

"Then he's late," he retorted with a cocky grin. "I'll keep you company until he gets here."

She shrugged, pretending to be amused. "Have it your way. My husband's a professional football player and he hates it when strange men hit on me," she lied. "Did I mention that he outweighs you by about a hundred pounds and has a nasty temper? Of course, if you don't care about your personal safety…"

If the cowboy had known anything about the Wyatts, he would have known that she not only wasn't married, she didn't have a man in her life who could even frown at him in disapproval. But he was already rising to his feet. Scowling at her, he growled, "Sorry for bothering you," and strode off.

Watching him head back to the bar, Elizabeth sighed in relief. Finally! Now if the rest of the cowboys would take the hint and leave her alone, she might be able to eat in peace.

Before she could turn her attention back to the menu, however, another cowboy walked through the front door and joined the crowd at the bar. The second her eyes met his, Elizabeth felt her heart stop in midbeat. John.

He'd known she was there—he'd spied the ranch pickup the second he'd turned into the bar and grill's parking lot. He wasn't surprised she'd come into town for dinner. He, too, had hated the idea of a lonely meal. So here they were, each alone at the same restaurant. If that wasn't fate, he didn't know what was. Not that he believed in that kind of thing, he reminded himself, but he wasn't a man to miss an opportunity to have dinner with a beautiful woman. Even if she was his boss and off-limits. It was just dinner!

He started toward her...only to realize that he wasn't the only one. A tall, dark-haired cowboy he recognized as one of the hands from the Double XX crossed to her in three strides. As John watched, she looked up at the newcomer with a dazed look and the half smile of a woman who just recognized her date.

Surprised. John stopped in his tracks and swore softly. She had a date? Why was he so surprised? Okay, so she hadn't been in town very long. That didn't mean she hadn't had time to meet people. She was a beautiful woman. She probably had cowboys tripping over her wherever she went.

Something twisted in his gut at the thought, and he was shocked to realize he was jealous. He'd never been jealous in his life! What the hell was wrong with him? The last thing he needed was a woman, especially one like Elizabeth Wyatt. She wouldn't even be talking to him if she knew his past, he thought grimly. What decent woman would?

Irritated with his thoughts, with himself for caring, he turned on his heel and returned to the bar. In the old days, he would have ordered a beer and told the bartender to keep them coming. Those days were gone.

"Iced tea," he told the bartender flatly, and never saw Elizabeth send the cowboy packing. He told himself he wasn't looking her way again, but then Elizabeth's date shouldered his way to the bar next to him and ordered a whiskey. Surprised, John glanced back at Elizabeth and found her sitting alone, frowning at the menu as the waiter waited for her order.

"Don't waste your time," the cowboy growled. "She claims she's waiting for someone."

John told himself he'd be wise to take the man's advice. Approaching her, getting any more involved with her than he already was, would be nothing but a waste of time. So he ordered a steak from the bartender, along with another glass of iced tea, and directed his attention to the television mounted on a shelf in a corner over the bar.

He was, he promised himself, staying right where he was.

When his food was set in front of him ten minutes later, however, he couldn't stop himself from taking a quick peak at Elizabeth. He wasn't surprised to discover that she, too, had received her food. Like him, she was all alone in the crowded bar.

"Don't even think about going there," he muttered to himself, but it was too late. Before he even knew what he was going to do, he'd picked up his plate and silverware and headed straight for her.

"Mind if I join you?"

Startled, Elizabeth looked up, and for a split second she started to smile. Then she realized how her heart was pounding and she stiffened. She knew she should send him back to the bar. She'd been aware of his every move from the moment he'd walked in and their eyes had met, and she was hurt he'd made no move to join her then. When had she given him the power to hurt her? Confused, worried, she reminded herself that she'd come to town because she needed to put some distance between them. She couldn't do that and have dinner with him.

She knew that, accepted it, and was shocked when she heard herself say, "Of course. Pull up a chair." *What was she doing?*

"I didn't come over when I first came in because I thought you had a date," he said casually as he took the seat across from her. "What happened? It must have been serious. I can't imagine any man standing you up for any other reason."

For a moment, Elizabeth was convinced she couldn't possibly have heard him correctly—he wasn't the kind of man who threw casual compliments around. But he looked up from his steak with a frown, obviously waiting for an answer, and she realized he wasn't the least bit casual. He was sincere.

Flushed, touched, she had no choice but to admit the truth. "I didn't have a date," she said huskily. "I just decided to come into town for dinner, and Buck told me this place was incredible."

"He was right," he said, taking another bite of his steak. "I'm surprised you eat beef. You seem more like a salad girl."

In the process of cutting another piece of steak, she burst out laughing. "Me? You must be joking! I love meat! When I found out my brother and sisters and I had inherited the ranch, I was thrilled! An unlimited supply of beef. Can you imagine? Life doesn't get any better than that."

John laughed. "I agree, but I would have never taken you for a carnivore. What else don't I know about you? C'mon," he teased when she hesitated. "You might as well tell me or I'll just make something up. What do you do for a living? You're a ballerina, right? Or maybe a doll maker? Or a musician in a rock band—"

"Yeah, right!" she chuckled. "I can't carry a tune to save my life. I'm a buyer for a dress shop in London."

"A buyer? Wow! No kidding? How'd you get into that?"

She shrugged, smiling. "I just sort of fell into it.

The father of one of my friends from school was a buyer for Harrod's, and he would take us with him sometimes when he went to fashion shows. That was all it took. I was hooked."

"Did you have any trouble getting off work for a month to stay here while Buck went on his honeymoon? Your boss couldn't have been very happy about that."

"No, but I had the leave. And I promised to check out the markets while I was here."

"That was a smart move on your part."

"I want to open a shop here with my sister when she gets out of design school," she admitted with a smile. "I need to know as much as I can."

"And what about the man you left behind? What does he think of you being gone for a month?"

He slid the question in so smoothly that it was several seconds before Elizabeth realized what he was asking. She should have said her private life was none of his business—after all, she *was* his boss—but the words just came tumbling out. "Oh, he was fine with it," she retorted. "He's a professional soccer player and he was going to Germany for a tournament. He promised he'd be waiting for me when I got back home."

His gaze narrowed at her less-than-sweet tone. "Why do I have the feeling he lied through his teeth?"

"Because he did," she said flatly. "He's with a blond groupie in Berlin. I saw his picture on the front page of a tabloid at the newsstand at Heathrow right before I caught my flight to the States. I hadn't even left home yet and he was already cheating on me."

"The man's an idiot."

She laughed without humor. "I know…*now.* Unfortunately, I thought he was the man I could spend the rest of my life with. Talk about lousy judgment."

Images flashed before his eyes of his ex-wife, his drinking and the trust he had destroyed. His ex probably felt the same way about him that Elizabeth felt about her former boyfriend, and he couldn't say he blamed her. All he'd cared about was himself.

"You weren't the first woman to make a mistake and trust the wrong man," he told her grimly. "Be thankful you found out who he was before you married him. You could have had a home and kids when you found out the truth."

"True," she agreed, grimacing. "Wouldn't that have been awful? I guess I should be thanking my lucky stars, shouldn't I?"

"You dodged a bullet. You should be celebrating. Let's go dancing when we finish eating."

The invitation surprised them both. Irritated with himself for pushing her, he almost told her to forget it—she was his boss, and he didn't want to put her on the spot. But before he could say a word, she said, "Country-western dancing? Like at Buck's wedding?"

He grinned. "Is there any other kind?"

"Oh, I'd love that! Where?"

"There's a dancehall at the north end of town. The same band that played at the wedding plays there every Wednesday night."

"Are you kidding? What are we doing here? Let's go!"

"What about your steak?" he laughed as she jumped to her feet. "You're not finished."

"I'll take it with me," she said, and signaled the waiter for the check.

Driving the Broken Arrow's pickup, Elizabeth followed John's Jeep to the Lazy Circle Dance Hall, then spent the next ten minutes trying to find a parking place. The lot was packed with pickups of every conceivable color and age, and nobody seemed to be leaving. Then, just when she thought neither she nor John was going to be able to find a place, two couples strolled out of the dance hall within seconds of each other. Just that quickly, they both had parking places.

Appearing at her side the second she stepped from the truck, John held out his hand to her. "Ready?"

For what? Dancing or something more? she

almost asked him, but she couldn't manage the words. Somehow the evening had turned into a date, and she knew that if she placed her hand in his, she was acknowledging that.

Every instinct she possessed screamed at her not to do it, but she knew in her heart that it was too late for that. The second he'd walked into the bar and their eyes met, she'd known that the evening had changed. Unable to stop herself, she placed her hand in his.

Without a word, she let him lead her into the dance hall.

Chapter 5

She wasn't in England anymore.

Watching cowboys two-stepping around the dance floor with their dates, the men in their pressed, creased jeans, and the women wearing everything from tight jeans and sparkling belt buckles to ruffled dresses that flowed with every turn, Elizabeth felt as if she was on the other side of a Western rainbow. And she loved it. She'd gotten a taste of it at Buck's wedding, but she'd thought that the dancing at the reception was something that the locals only did at special parties and receptions. Obviously, she couldn't have been more wrong.

"Well?"

Tearing her gaze away from the dancers, Elizabeth looked up at John with a grin. "Well, what?"

"Are you going to fish or cut bait?"

"Oh, I'm going to fish," she assured him with a flash of her dimples. "I'm just waiting for someone to ask me."

"Really? So you're the kind of woman who waits for a man to make the first move? How disappointing."

Another woman might have been fooled by his serious tone, but Elizabeth knew better. She saw the glint in his eye, the way the corner of his mouth twitched as he tried to hang on to his too somber expression. He was teasing her, daring her, and enjoying every second of it. So he didn't think she had the nerve, did he? Well, they'd see about that.

Making no effort to hold back a smile, she turned to survey the cowboys crowding the edge of the dance floor, waiting for a chance to dance with the first available woman who walked off the floor. "Well, let's see," she mused. "I love a tall man...and a lean build. And he's got to be attractive, of course. Not in a pretty-boy way. I like rugged, with dark hair. You see anyone like that?"

She hadn't fooled him anymore than he had her. Chuckling, he grabbed her hand. "Brat. C'mon, let's dance."

"I'd love to," she retorted, grinning. "Thank you so much for asking."

He pulled her out onto the dance floor, and within seconds, John sent her twirling away from him, only to bring her back again. Laughing, her head spinning and her feet moving in perfect timing with his, she learned to two-step, line dance, and do the cotton-eyed Joe. And she'd never had so much fun in her life.

She could have danced all night, but then the music turned soft and dreamy and the couples surrounding them pulled each other close and swayed to the strains of a country love song. Her eyes met John's, and suddenly, all she wanted to do was melt into his arms and give in to the need he'd been stirring in her all evening with just the touch of his hand.

It was time to go home.

"It's getting late," she said huskily.

"It's been a long day," he agreed. "We probably should call it a night."

He didn't want to let her go, didn't want to go back to being nothing more than boss and ranch foreman. For the first time in a long time, he'd forgotten the past, forgotten why no decent woman would want anything to do with him. He'd had a hell of a good time, and it was all because of Elizabeth. She'd shown him a side of herself she usually fought to keep under wraps—the fun, flirty, daring woman with mischief dancing in her eyes—and he hadn't been able to take his eyes off her. For hours, there'd been no sign of the boss, no sign of the woman nursing a broken heart who was determined to never be hurt again. She'd let herself go, and in the process, she'd knocked him out of his shoes.

He hated to see the evening end, but he knew she was right. It was time to call it a night…before he did something stupid. Like forget that she had the power to fire him…because that was the only thing that was keeping him from reaching for her again and kissing the stuffing out of her.

"C'mon," he said huskily. "I'll walk you to the truck, then follow you home."

The parking lot was surprisingly dark—the only light on was the one closest to the dance hall's side door. Surprised, Buck frowned at the other lights that marked the perimeter of the parking lot. They were all dark. "What happened to the lights? Weren't they all on when we first got here?"

"I thought they were. Maybe someone in the bar blew a fuse."

"Possibly," he agreed as they headed to the far corner of the lot where she'd left the truck. "Or a transformer blew for some reason. If that's the case, though, all the lights in the area would have gone out."

"I suppose someone could have shot out each of the parking lot lights with a pellet gun, but then the lights would have probably shattered." Dragging her eyes away from the dark lights, which looked perfectly fine, she glanced ahead to where the truck was parked in the distance. Something didn't look right. Frowning, she squinted in the darkness, searching the shadows that enveloped the vehicle. "What…oh, my God! My tires!"

John followed her gaze and swore roundly. Even from a distance, it was obvious that all four of the truck's tires were flat. "What the hell!"

"It's him, isn't it?" she cried as they rushed to the truck and discovered that all four tires had been slit. "The same sicko who left the note on my pillow! Why does he keep doing this? Is he following me? How else did he know I was here?"

"You don't know that it was him," he pointed out grimly. "Or that *him* is really a him."

"Okay, so we can't establish gender. But are you saying that this has nothing to do with the note in my bedroom? That someone else was driving past, saw the truck and decided to take their shot at scaring me into leaving town?"

"It's possible, Elizabeth," he said quietly. "We don't know how many people are after the ranch. It could be one, ten, thousands. All we can say for sure is that these aren't random acts of violence. They're deliberate. You're the target and there's a good possibility that the violence against you is going to get worse."

She paled at his words. "What if it wasn't someone driving past? What if someone in the dance-hall did this? Were we dancing right next to them? How could I not know that?"

"We don't know that whoever did this was someone inside," he assured her. "And don't beat yourself up over the fact that you might not recognize your enemies, even if they're standing right next to you. How could you? Apparently, half the residents of Colorado think they're Hilda's unnamed heir."

He was right, and that was what terrified her. How could she protect herself when she didn't know who to protect herself from?

Muttering a curse, John reached for his phone. "It's probably not going to do any good," he told her, "but I'm calling the police. We have to report this. And if we're lucky, somebody passing by saw something."

Ten minutes later it was obvious to both John and Elizabeth that the police couldn't do anything. After questioning a number of people at both the dance hall and the Rusty Bucket and not coming up with a single witness, there was little that Officer Petty, the young, baby-faced policeman who arrived on the scene with his lights flashing and siren blaring, could do to help.

"I'm sorry," he told them sincerely, "but with no witnesses, no evidence—"

"What about four slit tires?" John demanded, scowling. "If that's not evidence, I don't know what is."

"Of course it's evidence," the other man said patiently. "But we have no witnesses, we don't know what kind of knife was used, who did this, if they were on foot or in some kind of vehicle. We've got nothing," he stressed. "Nothing!"

"So, in other words, there's nothing you can do," Elizabeth said, cutting in. "Isn't that what you're saying?"

"No, ma'am," he replied. "I wish there was, but without any evidence or witnesses, I might as well try to catch a ghost. All I can do is keep my eyes and ears open. Maybe some kids did this. Summer's right around the corner, school's almost out—"

"This wasn't the work of kids and you know it," John said flatly.

"Probably not," he agreed. "But in the eyes of the law, you can't assume anything."

"Maybe you can't," John retorted, "but I sure as hell can. She's had a threatening note on her pillow in her bedroom, for God's sake! Tires slit, fences cut, cattle stolen. And that doesn't even touch the attacks against Buck and the ranch before he got married. If you can't see that someone is after the Wyatts, then you're blind as a bat."

Put on the spot, the younger man could only say, "The Wyatts have suffered a series of unfortunate events lately. Without witnesses or evidence, I can't do anything."

Furious, John knew he was right, but that only irritated him more. Somebody somewhere knew who was behind all the attacks, and it was up to the police to track them down. "Let us know if you find anything," he growled. "C'mon, Elizabeth, I'll take you home."

"What about the truck?"

"I'll call a wrecker service and have it taken to a garage in the morning for some new tires. Hopefully, we can get it back to the ranch before someone else decides to sabotage it."

Sitting quietly next to John as he turned north out of the parking lot, Elizabeth couldn't stop thinking about the hours she and John had spent dancing. She couldn't remember the last time she'd had so much fun, and that was the problem. In John's arms, she'd been totally oblivious to everything that was happening around her. Jack the Ripper could have been dancing right next to them, plotting her demise, and she would never have known it...because all she could see was John.

And that scared the hell out of her. How far would someone go to get their hands on the ranch? Would they be content to just scare her in the hope that she would leave before Buck returned? Or would they try to hurt her? Kill her? Make her pay for something Hilda had done when she'd written her will the way she had?

"You're awfully quiet," John said, shattering the dark stillness that had settled over them as he left the lights of Willow Bend behind and headed for the ranch. "Are you all right?"

"No," she said quietly. "I'm not."

"I'm not going to let anything happen to you."

"I know you mean that, but you can't make that kind of promise," she replied. "Look what happened tonight. We spent the last two hours dancing and having fun and didn't have a clue that someone in the crowd had a knife."

"You don't know that it was someone at the dance hall—"

"What if next time, whoever slashed my tires decides to use the knife on my throat? And I don't even know who it is?"

With a muttered curse, John pulled over and threw the transmission into Park. In the next instant, he was reaching for Elizabeth and pulling her into his arms. "That's not going to happen," he growled. "You're not going to get hurt because I'm not doing my job, not paying attention. Do you hear me? That's not ever going to happen again."

Pulling back slightly, she frowned up at him in the darkness. "What do you mean...*again?* When did someone get hurt because you weren't doing your job? You're so conscientious. I just can't imagine you ever being careless."

He should have told her everything then, but he didn't want to see the shock in her eyes. So he sugar-coated the truth and hated himself for it. "There was an accident when I was in the Navy," he said stiffly. "It was my fault, my watch."

She frowned, her eyes searching his. "Accidents happen—"

"I was a Navy SEAL, Elizabeth. Accidents aren't suppose to happen."

She wanted to argue with him, but his jaw was set, his eyes full of self-loathing, and her heart ached for him. How long had he been beating himself up for something that could have happened to anyone? She wanted to ask, but he had obviously said all he intended to say on the subject.

"I don't want you to be afraid," he said huskily. "I'm not going to let anything happen to you."

"I never thought you would," she told him quietly. "But my safety is my responsibility, too. I want you to teach me how to shoot a rifle."

In the process of putting the transmission back into Drive, he shot her a sharp look in the darkness. "You don't need to do that."

"Yes, I do. Rainey's a lot tougher than I am, and she was still nearly killed by the idiot who blew up the old Spanish mine."

"David Saenz is dead," he reminded her. "He can't hurt you or your family ever again."

"He was only a paid thug," she informed him. "The sheriff was never able to discover who hired him. So the jackass, whoever he is, is still out there, along with every other idiot who thinks he has a reason to be Hilda's unnamed heir. I don't know who my enemies are, John. I have to be able to protect myself."

"So, what are you saying?" he demanded. "You're going to start packing a gun everywhere you go now?"

"No, of course not. But I plan to watch my back. And when you're out repairing downed fences or taking care of the cattle and I'm at the house by myself, I'm going to have a gun within reach. Just in case. So are you going to teach me to shoot or not?"

"We'll start first thing in the morning," he told her. "I'll set up a target behind the barn. How does nine sound?"

"Great. I'll be there."

That problem settled, they had another one to settle when he pulled up in front of the house. The porch light was on, just as they'd left it, and the house looked as safe as a tomb. They both knew, however, that looks could be deceiving.

"Stay here while I check things out," he told her as he pulled up before the front door and cut the engine. "I'll be right back."

"Wait! You shouldn't—"

He was already gone, opening the front door with his spare key and stepping inside before she could stop him. Her heart pounding, Elizabeth shivered, feeling the touch of eyes upon her. But when she looked sharply around, she couldn't see anything but the darkness.

Suddenly afraid, she couldn't sit there another second. Pushing open the passenger door, she hurried across the front porch and rushed inside just as John stepped into the entrance hall. "Dammit, Elizabeth, you were supposed to stay in the truck!"

"I was scared—"

Swearing, he stepped past her and jerked open the door. "What happened?"

"Nothing!" she assured him. "I just…felt like someone was watching me. I didn't see anyone," she added quickly as she followed him outside onto the front porch. "I was just being paranoid."

"Hush," he said quietly. "Listen."

Snapping her teeth shut, she watched as he stared

out into the darkness, listening. The wind whispered through the pines, and far in the distance, the lonely call of a wolf echoed in the night. Nothing else moved.

"Why did you think someone was watching you?" he asked softly. "Did you hear something?"

Staring out at the darkness with him, she hugged herself. "No. I know it sounds crazy, but I could feel eyes on me, like someone was standing in the shadows watching me."

"Where? By the drive? At the end of the porch? Somewhere a hundred yards away with binoculars?"

"I don't know. Maybe from a distance. Like I said, I'm probably just being paranoid. After what happened tonight, I guess it's not surprising that I feel like I'm being followed or something. Who wouldn't?"

"Let's go back inside," he told her. "We need to talk about tonight."

"Tonight?" she asked with a frown as she followed him inside. "What about it?"

"I don't want you lying awake all night, waiting for some monster to jump out of the darkness at you," he said. "So I'm going to stay here at the house tonight. I'll sleep on the couch in the family room again."

Until that moment Elizabeth hadn't realized just how much she was dreading the moment when he went back to his cabin and she was left alone in the house for the night. "I probably should insist that that's not necessary, but I can't. Thank you."

"No problem," he said easily. "If you're the least bit nervous about anything, all you have to do is yell. I'm a light sleeper—I'll hear you."

"Are you sure you wouldn't rather sleep in the downstairs guest room? You'll be much more comfortable than on the couch."

"The guest room is at the back of the house—that's not going to work. I need to be close to the central hall to make sure no one breaks in and comes up the stairs."

Horrified, she said, "Do you think that's really going to happen?"

"It's not a question of what I think will happen—it's a matter of being prepared for anything."

"But how can you be? We don't know anything about whoever slit my tires and left a note on my pillow. We don't even know how many people are involved. How can you prepare for that?"

"You can't," he said simply. "All you can do is take steps to see that you have everything in place to protect yourself. That doesn't just mean having weapons and ammunition ready if someone attacks. You have to be aware of your surroundings, your vulnerability, at all times. You need to know escape routes, where the keys to the truck are, where your cell phone is, where I am.

And if we're both always on guard and we're damn lucky, that'll be enough to keep you safe."

"Because we can't depend on the police."

"Because we can't depend on the police," he repeated curtly. "It's not that the authorities don't want to do anything. With no evidence or witnesses, their hands are tied."

He painted a grim picture, one that shook her to the core…and infuriated her. "They're not going to get away with it, John," she vowed. "Whoever the hell *they* are, they're not going to get away with it. They're not going to drive me or my family away. The Broken Arrow is ours, not only by Hilda's will, but by birthright, and I don't give a damn who thinks they're entitled to it—they're not."

She sounded so fierce that John had to grin. "I guess you're not the pale English flower I thought you were."

"You're damn straight," she growled, then found herself fighting a smile. "Don't make me laugh. This infuriates me!"

"It should," he retorted. "If I were in your shoes, I'd be just as furious. You're chasing ghosts in the dark and getting nowhere. But don't worry, sooner or later, someone's going to mess up. And when they do, *everyone* will know who they are. And they won't be able to run fast enough, hard enough, to escape the judgment that's going to come down on their head."

She knew he was right. "I'll just be glad when our year probation is up and the ranch is rightfully ours. In the meantime, we just have to get from here to there."

"And you will," he assured her. "One day at a time, and this one's almost over. Why don't you go to bed? I'll lock up down here and watch over things."

"I can't," she said simply, giving him a grimace of a smile. "I'm too wound up. I'll never be able to sleep."

"Then how about a movie? I can pop one in the DVD player. I've got the latest Harry Potter movie. It might remind you of home."

She had to laugh at that. "Thanks, but no thanks. Hogwarts isn't exactly home. I'd rather go up in the attic."

Surprised, he lifted a dark male brow at her. "For what?"

"Just to explore. I stuck my head in there the other day, and you wouldn't believe what's stored up there! It looks like a museum...or an antique store. There's furniture up there that must have been in the family since the first Wyatt settled here. I just thought I'd go through it all, maybe bring some things downstairs and use them again."

"You want to do that *tonight?*"

"Why not?" she tossed back with a grin. "What else do we have to do?"

He could think of any number of things, all of

which included kissing her, none of which he would allow himself to do. She might have understood the *accident* he was responsible for in the Navy, but she didn't know the rest. And she wouldn't be nearly as understanding when she did. No woman who was looking for a man she could trust would.

"It looks like we're going up to the attic," he told her ruefully. "Lead the way."

"Oh, my God, look at this wardrobe!" she exclaimed ten minutes later as they pushed through the cobwebs to a collection of furniture that was covered in dust. "It doesn't have a scratch on it!"

He looked at her like she'd lost her mind. "Have you looked at that thing? It must weigh a ton. How the devil do you expect the two of us to get it downstairs?"

"There's a dolly over there," she said, nodding to the corner behind him. "We can get it to the stairs—"

He just looked at her. "And then what?"

She shrugged. "Then we carry it downstairs."

"Just like that? And who goes first, carrying the thing backward? Let me guess. That would be me."

She grinned sheepishly. "Well, you are stronger than I am, so it makes sense for you to take the heavy end."

"How did I know you would say something like

that?" he laughed. "C'mon, if we're going to move the damn thing, let's get started."

"Are you serious? You'll help me?"

"That depends on how long you stand here talking," he teased. "If you give me time to think about it, I just might change my mind."

Lightning quick, she stepped past him and grabbed the dolly. "Then let's get started. What do you want me to do?"

"Just guide me in the right direction when I'm going down the stairs backward."

"Oh, but don't you want me to lift one end or something?"

"Nope. I've got it."

"But—"

"I've got it, Elizabeth," he chuckled, and proved it by positioning the dolly under the bottom of the wardrobe, then leaning the piece backward so that all the weight was on the dolly and its two wheels. Within a matter of moments, he'd moved the wardrobe to the top of the stairs.

"Okay, we're going to go nice and slow," he assured her. "Ready? Okay, down we go."

Positioning herself at the opposite end of the wardrobe as he slowly started down the stairs, Elizabeth carefully guided him and held her breath the entire way. "Two more steps," she told him. "That's right. You're doing great. You're almost there. Thank God!"

"I couldn't agree more," he grunted. "Where do you want it?"

"In my bedroom." When he lifted a brow at her, she said, "Don't look at me like that. I think it matches my bed."

"Sure," he teased. "I know your kind. You just want to get me into your bedroom."

"You think so, do you?" she teased, and wondered how he knew, when she hadn't let herself even think such a thing…until now. "Actually, I want to get you into practically every room in the house. Now that I've had a chance to get a closer look at the things in the attic, there are at least six more pieces I want to bring downstairs."

"Tonight?"

She grinned. "Tonight."

"But shouldn't you talk to Rainey first? She and Buck will be living here—"

"The house belongs to all of us, and we all have our own suites. Anyway, Rainey loves anything old. She'll be thrilled. So as soon as we get this in place, we'll swap out the dining room table and buffet for the one in the attic. Okay?"

Left with no choice, all he could do was groan.

Chapter 6

"You're going to do what?"

"Make some pancakes," she said with a laugh. "I'm hungry."

"But it's three o'clock in the morning!"

"And we worked up an appetite." Surveying the antique dining room table and chairs that were now in their rightful place in the dining room, she smiled in satisfaction and rubbed her hand over the surface that was worn from decades of wear and was absolutely beautiful. "We need to break this baby in, and I can't think of a better way to do it than with pancakes."

His mouth watering at the thought, John had to agree with her. "There's probably a pancake mix around here somewhere—"

"Pancake mix?" she said, horrified. "Bite your tongue. I'll make them from scratch, silly." And without another word, she headed for the kitchen.

Following her, John expected her to find a recipe in one of the cookbooks that had belonged to Hilda, but she didn't even glance at the bookcase in the corner. Instead, she started assembling the necessary ingredients, and in the time it took to blink, the pancake batter was ready and she had the griddle heating on the huge antique gas stove that dominated the kitchen.

"Well," he said dryly, "you obviously don't need any help from me. I guess I'll set the table and put some coffee on. Or would you rather have tea?"

"Coffee," she said promptly. "I brought my own tea, but I'm rationing it."

"You're kidding."

She laughed sheepishly. "I know it sounds crazy, but there it is. Now you know. I'm a tea hoarder."

"I'll remember that," he said with a grin. "How are the pancakes coming?"

"Almost done," she said, and scooped up the last two on the griddle. Turning to him with a full platter of pancakes dripping in butter, she grinned. "I hope you're hungry. I'd hate to eat all of these by myself."

She was barely five-three and slender—he could easily span her waist with his hands—but he knew better than to be fooled by her size. He'd seen her eat like a lumberjack. "Four of those are mine, so don't even think about grabbing them for yourself," he warned teasingly. "I'd hate to have to wrestle you for them."

"You wouldn't dare."

The corners of his mouth curled wickedly. "You think not?"

For a moment he could see consideration glinting in her sapphire-blue eyes. Somewhere in the back of his head, he tried to remember why he couldn't take a chance with her or any other woman, but when she looked at him like that, all he could think about was kissing her.

A blush stole into her cheeks, but she didn't look away. "The food's getting cold," she reminded him huskily.

"Then we'd better eat," he rasped. But he didn't move, and neither did she.

Her heart pounding, Elizabeth told herself to move before he suspected that she couldn't, but it was too late for that. She was standing there staring at him like a ninny who'd never seen a man before. What must he be thinking?

The possibilities of that snapped her back to attention as nothing else could. "Is the coffee ready? If you'll carry these into the dining room, I'll heat the syrup in the microwave and grab the butter from fridge." Not giving him a chance to say a word, she shoved the platter of pancakes into his hands and quickly turned away.

If he noticed that she was moving around the kitchen like a whirlwind and didn't quite look him in the eye, he kept the thought to himself, thank God. Then it was time to eat, and both of them turned their attention to the food.

John took one bite and suddenly understood why a man could fall for a woman who knew how to cook. Startled, he looked up at her sharply. "You're a dangerous woman to have around."

Surprised, she laughed. "I beg your pardon?"

"I thought you were pulling my leg."

"Pulling your—" Suddenly realizing his meaning, she grinned. "You thought I was lying about being able to cook? I guess I shocked you."

"That's putting it mildly," he chuckled. "You look like a woman who wouldn't even know how to turn a stove on."

Far from offended, she studied him with twinkling eyes. "Do the women you know usually say they can do something they can't?"

"People say things all the time they don't expect

to get called on," he said with a shrug. "I had a friend who claimed he used to play football with the Minnesota Vikings. Then one day, the two of us were at a bar in Denver when we ran into one of his old teammates that he'd claimed he still kept in touch with. The second he saw the guy, he turned his back on him. When I called him on it, he admitted he'd never played pro ball—he didn't even play in college."

"That must have been incredibly awkward."

"That doesn't begin to describe it," he said with a grimace. "I felt damned uncomfortable, but I'm sure that was nothing compared to what he was feeling. He never spoke to me again."

"You're kidding! It wasn't your fault he lied."

"No, but every time he looked at me, he knew I knew he lied. I don't think he could handle it." His attention returning to his pancakes—or rather, the syrup that was left—he looked up at her with a grin. "The next time you tell me you know how to cook something, I'm grabbing a plate and fork. What's for breakfast?"

"This *was* breakfast," she laughed.

"Oh, no, you don't," he told her, grinning. "You're not going to get off that easy. That was a snack. We can't have breakfast until the sun comes up."

"Really? Where's that carved in stone?"

"In the kitchen," he said promptly. "One of your

ancestors must have carved that in the stone next to the old fireplace. Didn't you see it?"

Amused, she warned, "Watch it. You're starting to sound like your football-playing friend."

"Meow. Now you're getting nasty. And I thought you were so sweet."

"Yeah, right," she laughed. "Since when? We've been butting heads ever since the wedding."

"True," he agreed, chuckling. "But that's only because you think you're the boss."

"Don't start that—"

"And, of course," he added smoothly, "we both know you're not."

Sitting back in her chair, she studied him in amusement. "I'm not letting you push my buttons so easily this time."

He frowned with pretended innocence. "Push your buttons? Me? I don't have a clue what you're talking about."

"Watch it," she warned. "There's an antique Persian rug in the attic that's calling my name. If you bring it down to the living room, you can help me rearrange the furniture and decide where it looks best—"

"No!" he said quickly, horrified. "No more. I give. You're the boss. Give me orders all day long—I don't care as long as I don't have to move any more furniture. It's nearly four o'clock in the morning!"

"Poor baby," she teased. "Okay. You can call it a night. I'm going to do the dishes—"

"I'll help."

She should have told him no. There'd been too many times tonight when she'd completely forgotten his reason for spending the evening with her had nothing to do with whether he liked her or not. He was guarding her.

She wanted to ask him if the only reason he teased her was to distract her from the grimness of her situation, but she really didn't want to know the answer to that. Just the possibility that he was being nice to her because she needed his protection made her heart hurt.

"Hey, you all right?"

Pulled from her thoughts to find him studying her with a frown, she forced a quick smile. "Of course. But you don't have to help me. I know you're tired. Why don't you go to bed? I can finish these up by myself."

"Nope," he said easily. "You cooked. I'll do the dishes while you go relax in the family room." And not giving her time to argue further, he shooed her out of the kitchen and started loading dirty dishes into the dishwasher.

Ten minutes later, John turned out the lights in the kitchen and stepped into the family room. Expecting

Elizabeth to be plotting her next furniture move, he stopped in surprise at the sight of her asleep on the couch. He only had to look at her to know that she hadn't planned to fall asleep. Her feet were on the floor, her head propped in her hand, and a magazine was open on her lap. She couldn't have been comfortable, but she'd run out of gas, and her body had obviously shut down the second she sat for a few minutes.

He shouldn't have gone anywhere near her, but how was he supposed to resist her when she looked so beautiful? He'd never seen her so relaxed, so trusting, so damn sexy. Just looking at her made him ache.

You're asking for trouble, you idiot. Get the hell out of there before you do something stupid.

He turned to walk out, only to remember why she was downstairs at that hour of the morning in the first place. She hadn't fooled him when she'd insisted on moving furniture in the middle of the night. She was scared, dammit, and that infuriated John. He hoped whoever was terrorizing her was enjoying himself, because his days were numbered. When John discovered who he was, he was going to wish he'd never been born.

Silently crossing to the couch, he soundlessly removed the magazine from her lap, then grabbed a pillow and slipped it under her head. Sighing softly, she shifted in her sleep, drawing her feet up to the couch and stretching into a more comfortable position. John felt something tighten in his chest and told himself it wasn't his heart. He didn't have one anymore. But as he took a throw from the back of the couch and spread it over her, he couldn't deny that she tugged at his emotions in a way he hadn't expected.

If he'd had any sense, he would have taken up a position in the hall to protect her, somewhere out of sight of Sleeping Beauty on the couch. Instead he dropped down into the easy chair across from her and stared at her broodingly. What the devil was he going to do about her? She was as much his boss as Buck was and the last woman on earth he should even be thinking about kissing, let alone making love to. But there it was, like it or not. All he could think about was kissing her, carrying her upstairs to bed and driving them both crazy, and he didn't have a clue what he was going to do about it.

The only thing he did know for sure was that he wasn't leaving her unprotected. If he had to sit and watch her all night in order to keep her safe, then by God, that's what he was going to do. Stretching his legs out in front of him, he leaned back in his chair and never took his eyes from her.

The dream was so real that he didn't even question whether he was awake or not. Elizabeth was there with him, in the hayloft, smiling at him in a way that heated his blood, her eyes full of promise as she reached for him. Damn, she was beautiful. And her skin was so soft. A man could lose himself in a woman who was that soft, he thought with a silent groan. All he had to do was give in to the need that was clawing at him like sharpened talons. Touch her. Kiss her. Make love to her until she screamed his name in ecstasy—

"John?"

Somewhere in the back of his mind the thought registered that he must be dreaming. But then Elizabeth called his name again, and it was impossible to tell where the dream ended and awareness of her began. He opened his eyes to find her leaning over him with a gentle smile that turned him inside out, and without a thought, he reached for her and pulled her onto his lap and into his arms.

"John! You're dreaming!"

"If I am," he growled, "I don't ever want to wake up." And with no more warning than that, his mouth closed over hers and he slipped back into the fantasy that had been teasing him for days.

He kissed her with a slow-burning hunger that sparked an ache low in her belly. With a soft moan, she melted against him, loving the taste of him on her tongue. He was dreaming—she'd known it the minute he'd opened his eyes and reached for her—

and she should have stopped him. But merciful heavens, the man could kiss! And when he pulled her close and wrapped his arms around her as though he would never let her go, she felt like *she* was the one who was dreaming. With a sigh, she melted against him and told herself that she wasn't going to let things get out of hand. Any second now, she was going to bring them both to their senses.

But then his hands moved over her, tracing the curve of her hip, her waist, the fullness of her breast, and her breath caught in her lungs. Her thoughts scattered. The world—the universe—vanished into thin air, and there was nothing but John and the hot mindlessness of his kiss.

Another woman might not have realized the exact moment when John came to his senses, but Elizabeth knew immediately. Somewhere in the bowels of the house, the grandfather clock struck six in the morning, and although John continued to kiss her, there was something in his touch, his kiss, that was...different.

With infinite slowness, he ended the kiss and pulled back far enough so he could study every inch of her face. "If you want to slap my face, I won't stop you. In my own defense, I thought I was dreaming."

She smiled slightly. "I know. So did I."

"How—"

"I woke up and saw you asleep in the chair and was just going to wake you and tell you I was going upstairs for a shower," she said. "I didn't want you to wake up and think someone had grabbed me or something..."

"And then I grabbed you," he said wryly when she hesitated. "I'm surprised you didn't knock my head off."

"You didn't know what you were doing," she pointed out as she climbed off his lap and turned to face him. "It could have happened to anyone."

"Maybe," he said with a shrug, "but I promise you that it won't happen again."

Not while he was asleep, anyway, he told himself silently. If he kissed her again, he was, by God, going to be wide awake. If he got fired, so be it. It would be worth it.

Rising to his feet, he added, "A shower sounds like a good idea. I thought I'd go back to my cabin, but I don't want to leave you here in the house unprotected."

"You can use the shower in Buck's suite," she told him. "It's right next to mine. If anything happened and I needed you, you'd be close enough to hear me if I called out. Not that I expect to have any problems," she assured him quickly. "All the exterior doors are locked, of course, and my bedroom door has a lock on it. I should be fine."

He knew she was probably right—the odds of

someone breaking in and hurting her when he was right next door were slim to none—but he hated the idea of leaving her alone, even if he was going to be right next door.

"I'll still feel better if I wait in the hall outside your suite while you take your shower," he told her gruffly. "Then you can go with me to my cabin while I clean up. Then I'll teach you to shoot."

"But—"

"No buts, Elizabeth. I'm not leaving you alone, so you might as well get used to the fact that I'm going to shadow your every move until whoever is threatening you is caught or Buck comes home and you go back to England. If you have a problem with that—"

"I can fire you?"

A wicked challenge glinting in his eye, he merely looked at her, a half smile curling one corner of his mouth. "What do you think?"

What she thought was the man had no business looking so darn sexy. When he smiled at her, and his dark brown eyes locked with hers, he made her want—

Something you can't have, the voice of reason retorted in her head. *Remember? You're done with men, love, all that garbage about happily ever after. The only thing you're looking for is a location for the shop you and Priscilla are going to open. You don't need a man for that.*

"What I think," she said huskily, "is that I'm going to take my shower now. If you want to stand guard in the hall, I can't stop you."

Her nose in the air, she sailed out, leaving him to follow, smiling. He wasn't, however, smiling when he paced the hall in front of her suite and found himself imagining her…in the shower naked.

Thirty minutes later, John stood under a cold shower in his cabin while Elizabeth waited for him in his small living room, but the cold water didn't help. Nothing did. When Elizabeth had stepped out of her bathroom after her shower, dressed in jeans that hugged her slim hips and a red T-shirt that made his mouth go dry, he'd just barely swallowed a groan. Then the intoxicating scent of her reached out to him, wrapping around him, stirring his senses, and he'd known he was in trouble.

A smart man would have called off the shooting lesson. But if there was one thing Elizabeth needed to know, it was how to handle a gun. And not just because she was being threatened. If she was going to be a rancher, she needed to be able to shoot, to protect herself, to kill, if necessary. And for no other reason than that, he was going to teach her to handle a gun. Without kissing her! It wasn't going to be easy.

Resigned, he finished his shower, then, as soon as

he dragged on jeans and a denim shirt, he joined her in his living room. "Okay," he growled, "let's get this show on the road...unless you'd rather do this later, when you're more rested. You need to be alert when you handle a gun."

"Oh, I am," she assured him. "The shower helped—and I did get a couple of hours sleep."

He had to admit that the lack of sleep didn't seem to have slowed her down at all. Her eyes were bright, her smile brighter, and she looked ready for anything. "Okay, let's get started then," he said, and pulled open the cabin door so she could precede him out onto the porch.

That, he realized almost immediately, was a mistake. He couldn't take his eyes off the sway of her hips. Swallowing a groan, he turned away to grab some empty soup cans he kept around for target practice, then strode over to a fence thirty yards away and set the cans on the top rail.

"This is a Winchester 94," he said, picking up the rifle he'd retrieved from the gun case in his cabin. "This one was my grandfather's and it's the first gun I learned to shoot. There's one in the gun cabinet in Buck's office that belonged to your great-grandfather."

Surprised, she looked up at him sharply. "And it still works?"

He grinned. "You won't find a ranch in this neck

of the woods that doesn't have a Winchester in the gun cabinet. They're damn good guns. They even used them in the production of *The Rifleman.*" When she just looked at him blankly, he groaned, "Don't tell me you never heard of *The Rifleman.* It was a television show back in the sixties—a Western. I think you can still catch it on cable—"

"I'm sorry," she said with a wry grimace. "I don't watch much television, and if it was ever broadcast in England, I never saw it."

"So how much experience do you have with guns?"

"None."

"Why? Because you're afraid of them?"

She considered the question with a frown. "No, I wouldn't say that, but then again, it's hard to say when I've never even held a gun before, let alone shot one. I guess time will tell."

"It's better to know now than when you find yourself in a situation when you need to protect yourself," he retorted. "So…step one. Always start with safety."

He showed her where the safety was, how to check the gun to make sure it was unloaded, where to load it, how to send a bullet into the chamber, then pull back the hammer before squeezing the trigger. "It's important to know your gun," he told her. "You want to be comfortable with the trigger, to know how much pressure you need to exert to make it fire, if it's a hair trigger—"

The words were hardly out of his mouth when she fingered the trigger and the hammer clicked back into place. If there'd been a bullet in the chamber, the gun would have fired.

"Oh, my God!"

"That's why you have to be careful," he said quietly. "I know of people who've been shot and killed just that easily, cleaning their own gun."

Horrified, Elizabeth would have liked nothing more than to hand him the gun and never touch it again, but he was right. She had to know how to protect herself. "I'll be careful," she assured him gruffly. "Now what?"

"You load it and try to knock one of the cans off the fence." Handing her a bullet, he watched as she placed it in the chamber. "It'll hold up to six bullets," he told her, "but I want you to practice loading it, so we're only going to put in one at a time. It's also safer. Okay, take your best shot."

Elizabeth frowned at the cans lined up on the fence rail. They suddenly looked like they were a mile away. Glancing at John, she said, "You're joking."

"It's not as difficult as it may look," he chuckled. "Here...let me help you."

She expected him to take the gun from her and

show her how it was done. Instead, he stepped close behind her and surrounded her with his arms and chest as he showed her how to hold the gun. "There's no scope," he said quietly in her ear as he molded her hands around the gun. "Now you just look down the barrel and line up the sight with the can. Got it?"

Her heart thundering in her chest, Elizabeth almost laughed. He couldn't be serious. How could he possibly expect her to be able to concentrate on a can thirty yards away when he was pressed so close she could feel every breath he took? "N-no," she said shakily, only to gasp when she suddenly had a can right in her sights. "Wait! Yes! Right there!"

"Good girl," he crooned in an incredibly seductive voice. "Now gently pull back the trigger. That's it. Make sure you have the can in your sights, then *gently* squeeze the trigger."

Her heart slamming against her ribs, she carefully inched her finger onto the trigger, held her breath and squeezed. Thirty yards away, not a single can moved.

Still pressed against her back, John chuckled. "You closed your eyes, didn't you?"

Surprised, she gasped, "How did you know?"

"Just a hunch." Dropping his arms from around her, he stepped back. "Now that you've got the hang of it, try it again. And this time, keep your eyes open."

Color climbed into her cheeks—did he have a clue how right his arms had felt around her?—she forced herself to focus. It wasn't easy. He watched her every move as she once again loaded a single bullet into the rifle, and when she turned her attention to the target, she could still feel the touch of his eyes. Concentrating, she stared unblinkingly at the can she had her sites on.

Don't blink. Don't blink. The refrain echoing over and over in her head, she squeezed the trigger…and sent the can flying into the air.

For a second she couldn't believe it. Then she laughed. "Oh, my God. I did it! I did it!" Whirling, she turned to throw herself into his arms.

Before she could do anything but take a step, their eyes met and suddenly awareness set the air humming between them. Did he know how badly she wanted to touch him? Kiss him? Did he feel the same? Her senses spinning, the ache in her heart turning to a need she refused to put a name to, she hesitated, her eyes searching his. If he'd given her one clue that he wanted her as much as she wanted him, she would have stepped forward in an instant.

But he didn't.

Chapter 7

By unspoken agreement, they decided to avoid each other the rest of the day and evening. Neither, however, had forgotten the threat to Elizabeth and the ranch, so John stayed within shouting distance. Elizabeth cooked dinner, but when she asked him if he'd like to join her, he put her off with the excuse that he had some paperwork to do in Buck's office and would eat while he worked. Telling herself it was for the best, she ate in front of the television in the family room and spent the next few hours searching the satellite channels for *The Rifleman.* She never found it.

By the time she went to bed, she was tired and

lonely, and she couldn't think of anything but John. She seemed to have radar where he was concerned. Listening to his nearly soundless movements in the house, she knew exactly where he was. After a rough night on the couch, she'd convinced him to sleep in Buck's room instead of downstairs, and at some point, she heard the sound of his footsteps on the stairs and in the hall as he strode past her room. Minutes later, a quiet stillness settled over the house.

If she slept that night, she had no memory of it. For what seemed like hours, she found herself listening for any sound of movement from the room next door. Silence echoed in her ears, but still, she couldn't sleep. By the time she heard John stir again, it was going on six, and she was exhausted.

Groaning, she rolled out of bed and stumbled into the bathroom for a hot shower to clear her head, but she couldn't say later how long she stood under the pounding water. When the fuzziness fogging her brain finally lifted, all she knew was that she couldn't keep hanging around the house, dreaming about John. She had to get out, put some space between them, find something else to think about.

Her shop.

The thought came to her as she was washing her hair and she immediately knew it was the perfect answer. She'd drive to Aspen or Vail, see what shop space was available, then check out the competition. Both towns were miles from Willow Bend and the Broken Arrow, and there wasn't a soul at either resort who would recognize her. She'd be safe, and if she was lucky, she wouldn't give John a thought all day.

Pleased with herself, she quickly rinsed her hair, then finished her shower. As soon as she was dressed, she grabbed the Jeep keys from the spot where they hung by the back door and hurried outside. The pickup, with its four new tires, was scheduled to be delivered to the ranch later in the morning, but she had no intention of hanging around the house that long.

The truck was parked in its usual parking spot, and John was nowhere in sight. Relieved, she slid behind the wheel and inserted the key in the ignition, her imagination already jumping ahead to the day she and Priscilla opened their own shop. She'd call her later and tell her what she'd found. The shop had to have great windows in the front. She could see them now. Priscilla would decorate them, of course. She had such a good eye for that—

"Where the devil do you think you're going?"

Startled, she nearly jumped out of her skin when John suddenly appeared right beside her and jerked open the driver's door. "You scared me!"

"You need to be scared," he growled. "Where do you think you're going?"

Indignation sparked in her eyes. "I beg your pardon?"

"Don't look at me like that," he retorted. "Have you forgotten what happened the last time you went out by yourself? Someone's after you—"

"That's why I'm going to Aspen," she told him. "I need to find space for the dress shop I plan to open, and no one knows me there."

"How do you know you won't be followed?" he pointed out. "You could be attacked before you get there, when no one's around to help you. Have you thought of that? How vulnerable you would be?"

"I would know if someone was following me—"

"Oh, really? You didn't even know I was right beside the truck until I spoke. What if I'd wanted to hurt you? I could have slit your throat before you could do anything but gasp."

She paled at the thought. As much as she hated to admit it, he was right. She'd let her guard down. That didn't mean she had to be locked up at the ranch like a prisoner. "Okay, so I wasn't thinking. I'll be more careful in the future. There. Satisfied?"

"No."

"Too bad. I'm getting out of here, and there's not a damn thing you can do about it."

"You think not?"

"I mean it, John. Get out of my way."

"Not a chance," he said grimly. "I told you last night that I was sticking close until Buck gets back and I meant it. You can forget about going off by yourself. It's not going to happen."

"Then you'd better climb in. I'm leaving."

She leaned forward to turn the key in the ignition, but John was quicker. In the blink of an eye, he jerked the keys out of her hand and dropped them into his pocket.

"Dammit, John!"

"Wait right here," he growled. "I'm going to my cabin to change. I'll be back in ten minutes."

"You can't go. You have to stay here so no one sabotages the ranch."

"I'm more concerned about you and someone hurting you to keep you away from the ranch."

"I'll be here—"

Not once glancing back, he ignored her efforts to discourage him and said, "I'm going to make sure of it. See you in ten, sweetheart."

Fuming, she glared after him, only to catch sight of herself in the rearview mirror. She looked like a two-year-old on the verge of a temper tantrum. This, she thought with a reluctant grin, was what the man had reduced her to. What was she going to do with him?

Images popped into her mind—hot, steamy, intimate images that set her heart pounding and her body aching. Groaning, she stiffened. The last thing she needed was to spend more time with him, but he was right—she had no business going off by herself. It just wasn't safe. So, like it or not, she was just going to have to find a way to deal with him.

He didn't make it easy for her. Ten minutes later, when he returned just as he'd promised, the scent of his cologne teased her senses when she scooted across the bench seat to the passenger's side and yielded the steering wheel to him. She had no business driving, anyway, she silently acknowledged to herself. She'd never be able to concentrate with him sitting right beside her.

If he had that same problem, he showed no sign of it. It wasn't until he left the ranch behind that she realized why. He kept checking the mirrors to make sure they weren't being followed, and she found herself doing the same thing.

"No one's following us," she said quietly.

"Let's hope it stays that way," he replied, and turned his attention back to the road.

Miles passed, and though they weren't the only vehicle on the road, the other cars and trucks that joined them on the road eventually turned off or passed them. If they were being followed, then whoever was tracking them was damn clever.

Glancing over at John, she said, "What do you think? Are we in the clear?"

Once again, his eyes lifted to the rearview mirror. "Probably, but the worst thing either one of us can do is underestimate whoever's after the ranch. There's too much at stake."

She had to agree. "Thanks for coming with me," she said. "You were right. I shouldn't have tried to go off by myself."

"What was that?" he asked, casting her a sharp look. "I think I must have misunderstood you. Did you say I was right? You couldn't have. My ears must have deceived me."

She laughed—she couldn't help herself. "I'm not that bad!"

"Really? Who didn't think I needed to stand guard in the hallway light night? Who thought I didn't need to sleep on the couch the night you found the note on your pillow? Who—"

"Okay, okay," she chuckled, cutting him off. "You win. I was totally and completely wrong. There. Is that what you wanted me to say?"

"Well, actually, I had in mind, 'Yes, John. Whatever you say, John. You're so smart, John. I don't know what I would do without you, John.'"

"Yeah, right," she laughed. "Try again."

"Damn. I was afraid you would say that."

When he returned his attention to the curving road that stretched out before them, she couldn't take her eyes off him. She'd missed not seeing him yesterday after the shooting lesson, not talking to him after they'd had so much fun moving furniture the night before. "Why have you been avoiding me? Was it something I said?"

She hadn't meant to ask. The words just popped out. Heat coloring her cheeks, she said quickly, "I'm sorry. Forget I said anything—"

"I wanted to kiss you."

He could have knocked her over with a feather. "So why didn't you?"

It was a simple question, and the answer should have been equally simple. Instead, he looked at her as if she'd lost her mind. "*Why?* Do you even have to ask? You're my boss, for God's sake! If you think I would have a relationship with someone who signs my paycheck, you don't know me very well."

So he was thinking of having a relationship? When? And what did being his boss have to do with anything?

Questions stumbling through her mind, she looked at him in confusion. "You can't be serious. First of all, I don't sign your paychecks—Buck does. And me being one of your bosses is irrelevant."

"The hell it is!"

He was furious...and obviously, more than a little

frustrated. Amazed, she tried to reason with him. "We're both adults, John. I'll be the first to admit that I've pulled rank on you but only because you try to pull it on me. But when it comes to…I don't care…"

Dragging his gaze from the road, he shot her an arch look. "What exactly are you trying to say?"

Heat climbing in her cheeks, she couldn't believe he was so dense. "What I'm trying to say," she blurted out in frustration, "is I don't get hung up on people's job positions. Not that it matters," she said quickly, before he could jump to the conclusion that she wanted him to kiss her, "because I don't plan to have a relationship with anyone right now. That would be crazy. I'm starting a new business and I don't have a clue where. That's the only thing that's important to me right now."

"Fine," he said flatly. "Then we have an understanding."

She told herself that this was a conversation they should have had days ago. Everything was spelled out—they were clear. She should have been relieved. So why did she feel like crying?

Aspen was everything Elizabeth had hoped it would be. There was no snow, of course, in the middle of May, but the town was teaming with tourists. It was the shops, however, that Elizabeth couldn't take her eyes off. There were wine shops, cigar bars, jewelry stores and delectable pastry shops that rivaled the best that Europe had to offer. It was, however, the clothing boutiques that dotted the shopping district that drew her eye. Nothing she saw in the shop windows rivaled the dresses she bought in London on a regular basis. And there wasn't anything remotely like the dresses Priscilla was designing.

"You realize you look like a kid in a candy store, don't you?"

Not realizing until then that John was watching her, she tore her gaze away from the shops they were passing and grinned at him. "It shows?"

"Only when your tongue hangs out."

"It does not!" she laughed.

"And then there's the way your tail wags—"

"John!"

"Of course, you haven't jumped out the window yet, so I guess you haven't completely lost all control."

Trying not to grin and failing miserably, she lifted a delicately arched brow at him. "Are you in any way implying that I'm a dog?"

"Moi? Never!"

"That's what I thought," she chuckled. "Okay, so I'm excited. I can't help it. My sister and I have talked about opening our own shop for years, and now that we've got the ranch, Colorado seems like the place to be…if we can find a store front we can afford."

"Then you might want to rethink Aspen. It's pricey. And there are other ski resorts that are more reasonable. We can check them all out if you like."

"I'd love to! Oh, stop here!" she said, suddenly noticing a shop with whispy dresses in the window. "I need to go in here."

He pulled into a parking space halfway down the block, and within minutes, Elizabeth was browsing through the shop, checking the merchandise for quality and style, not to mention price. She really hadn't expected John to follow her inside, but when she looked up from a sexy little black dress she was examining, there he was, standing by the door.

Another man would have looked like a fish out of water, but John seemed far from uncomfortable. In fact, he seemed right at home. He was examining the jewelry at the counter and talking to one of the sales girls about a set of earrings and a matching bracelet.

"Aren't they gorgeous!" Smiling prettily at him, the clerk held out the earrings for him to see. "They'd make a wonderful birthday present," she told him. "Or maybe something for your anniversary. Your wife—"

"I'm not married."

"Okay," she said easily, "then your girlfriend. I'm sure she would love it."

When his gaze lifted to Elizabeth's, the clerk

followed his gaze and smiled. "Oh, so she's here. Hi," she called to Elizabeth. "That's so nice that the two of you go shopping together. My boyfriend runs the other way when I even mention the *S* word."

Blushing, Elizabeth said, "Oh, we're not dating—"

"She always says that," John cut in. "Just because we're living together..."

"John!"

"She's old-fashioned," he told the clerk with a grin. "She doesn't like it when I tell people—"

She was, Elizabeth decided, going to kill him...it was just a matter of how. "Excuse us," she told the clerk, and strode across the shop to grab his hand and pull him outside. "What are you doing?"

"I don't know what you're talking about," he said innocently. "I was just telling the clerk—"

"I heard what you told her. What I want to know is why would you lead her to believe that?"

"Because we are."

"No, we're not!"

"You're address is the Broken Arrow Ranch and so is mine," he pointed out. "You sleep upstairs and so do I."

"But not together," she argued. "She thinks—"

"What she thinks is that we're a couple shopping together. She doesn't have a clue that you were scouting out your competition."

"Yes, but—" Suddenly realizing he was right, she felt like he'd hit her in the head with a brick. "*That's* why you said those things? Why didn't you say so?"

"Well, I couldn't very well say it in front of her," he chuckled. "It just seemed like a good idea at the time. I didn't mean to make you uncomfortable."

"You caught me off guard," she admitted huskily. "But it was a good idea. Thank you."

"My pleasure," he said with a smile. "So where to next?"

"The shop across the street," she said. "C'mon, let's go while the traffic's clear." And taking his hand, she pulled him after her across the street.

Caught up in the feel of her fingers in his, he expected her to release his hand when they stepped into the next shop, and she did...only to link her arm through his. "Look, honey," she purred in a perfect Southern accent. "They've got those push-up bras you just love. Wanna buy me one?"

Paybacks were, John decided with a grin, hell.

After that, they got caught up in the spirit of pretending. As the day progressed, they found themselves holding hands without even thinking twice about it as they went in one shop after another, completely forgetting that they were only supposed to be checking out dress shops. They looked at jewelry and antiques and Christmas decorations and everything in between. And when they finally headed back to the pickup, they were still holding hands.

"Are you hungry?" John asked her as he opened the door for her. "There's an Italian restaurant on the way home that's got the best pizza this side of the Rockies."

"Sounds good," she said. "Do you think they have chicken ranch?"

In the process of shutting her door for her as she buckled up, John froze. "*Chicken ranch?* Are you serious?"

"Well, yes," she said, surprised. "What have you got against chicken ranch?"

"Nothing. It's my favorite pizza."

It was her turn to look stunned. "You're joking."

"No, I'm not," he said seriously.

Over the course of the next few hours, he wished he was. When they stopped for pizza, the conversation somehow drifted to the subject of war and global politics and conservation. And even though they didn't agree on every subject, John had to admit that her views were damn fascinating.

She was fascinating.

He kept telling himself that they weren't out on a date, but he'd never spent an evening with a woman that felt more like a date. And that could lead to nothing but trouble.

He'd lost his mind, he decided. That was the only

logical explanation. If he had any sense, he would end this pretend game they were playing and remind her of the conversation they'd had that very morning, the very same one in which she'd made it clear that she had no intention of getting involved with anyone in Colorado because the only thing she was interested in was opening her dress shop. But he didn't want her to remember. Hell, *he* didn't want to remember. He just wanted to kiss her.

Afraid he was going to do just that, he was ready to leave the second they finished the last of the pizza. "We really need to be going," he told her. "We still have a long drive ahead of us, and I don't know about you, but I didn't get much sleep last night. I don't want to chance falling asleep on the drive home."

"Oh, of course," she said quickly, reaching for her purse. "If you're tired—"

"No!"

"Well, you don't have to turn me down so fast. I'm not that bad a driver."

"I never said you were," he retorted with a quick grin. "I just want to make sure we make it home in one piece."

"Now you're getting nasty."

She might have fooled him into thinking she was upset if he hadn't seen the twinkle in her eyes. "Have you seen the way you drive?" he teased. "Think about it. Would you want to ride with you?"

Fighting a smile, she sniffed, "Fine. Do all the driving. See if I care."

"Sounds good to me," he said, chuckling, and slipped behind the wheel.

The ride home was the exact opposite of the drive to Aspen. There was no worries about being followed, no long silences. They talked about Elizabeth's plans for her shop, when she planned to have it up and running, and other resort areas where she might do just as well. The time just seemed to fly by. And John still wanted to kiss her.

More than a little frustrated, he told himself he was going to put as much distance as possible between them when he got home, only to remember that he couldn't let her out of his sight. As long as she was in danger, he was going to stick to her like glue, even if she was driving him crazy.

His thoughts on her, he was ten miles from home before he noticed the yearling in the field that ran along the highway. It was nearly dark, and at first, he thought the year-old calf was just lying down in the pasture, taking it easy. Then he realized it was slumped over and not moving.

"Son of a bitch!" Swearing, he pulled over, checked his rearview mirror, then made a quick U-turn and came to a stop with his headlights trained on the pasture. There, not far from the fence, lay a dead calf. Its throat and stomach were ripped open, and blood was everywhere.

At his side, Elizabeth blanched. "Oh, God!"

"This is the third killing in a week," John said grimly.

"What could kill a calf that big?"

"A mountain lion. I was hoping it had moved on, but I should have known better. The calves are too tempting and easy pickings this far from the house."

Elizabeth couldn't bear to look at the poor dead calf—she didn't want to even imagine its awful death. Glancing at John, she studied him in the soft glow of the dash lights. "What are you going to do?"

"Find it and kill it," he retorted coldly. "We'll leave in the morning with the dogs."

Her heart stopped in midbeat at his words. "What do you mean...*we'll* leave?"

"You wanted to know everything about running a ranch," he reminded her. "Unfortunately, this is part of it."

She knew he was right, but the bottom dropped out of her stomach just at the thought of hunting down a mountain lion. If it could rip the throat out of a calf, what could it do to her?

Peering through the growing darkness, she could have sworn she could feel the lion staring at her, waiting to pounce. Cold chills danced over her skin. "Is it still out there?"

Turning the truck around, he didn't even bother to look. "No. Cats don't stay out in the open. They only stick around long enough to feed, then head back up into the mountains."

"But what about the calf?" she asked when he pulled back onto the road. "Shouldn't we do something?"

"There's nothing we can do," he retorted, "except leave it for the scavengers."

"But won't the cat come back for it?"

"Not usually. Why should it when there's plenty of fresh meat available?"

He had a point. Suddenly cold to the bone, she hugged herself as they raced toward the Broken Arrow's main entrance. "So what's the procedure for tomorrow?"

"We'll come back here with the dogs and horses in the morning and find the cat's scent," he told her as they reached the main entrance. "Then it's just a question of the horses keeping up with the dogs. They'll track it up into the mountains and corner it either in some trees or in a canyon somewhere. It won't be pretty," he warned her. "A cornered cat is about as unpredictable as a rattlesnake and twice as deadly. Maybe you shouldn't go. I certainly wouldn't blame you if you didn't."

"No, I want to go," she insisted.

"It's rough country."

"I can handle it."

"Even the kill? They're beautiful animals. You won't enjoy seeing one killed."

"I can handle it," she assured him. "This is my ranch, John. I wasn't kidding when I said I need to know everything about it. What if I was somewhere on the property by myself and I came across a mountain lion? I wouldn't have a clue what to do."

"The odds of you seeing one are slim to none," he retorted. "I've lived out west all my life, and the only time I've ever seen a mountain lion is when we had to track one down."

He was giving her an out, and there was a part of her that knew she should take it. But deep in the heart of her was her Wyatt blood urging her to go, claim what was hers, experience something she'd never dreamed of.

"I still want to go," she insisted. "What time are we leaving?"

"Six. I won't wake you up," he warned. "If you're not downstairs when I'm ready to leave, I'm leaving without you. Understood?"

She nodded. "I'll be ready."

Dawn was clear and cool, and Elizabeth was ready long before she heard John stirring next door.

Already dressed in jeans, boots and a long-sleeved cotton shirt, she was waiting in the foyer when John came downstairs. His expression somber, he said, "So you haven't changed your mind."

It was a statement, not a question. "I packed some sandwiches and water in case we're gone awhile," she said. "And I brought a jacket for the mountains. Do we need anything else?"

"Just the horses and the dogs. And the guns and ammo, of course," he added. "You'll be carrying a loaded rifle—"

"On horseback?" she asked, horrified. "Are you serious?"

"That's the only way you're going," he retorted coolly. "You don't get a vote on this, Elizabeth. If you have a gun, you at least have a way of protecting yourself. Without it, you could be a sitting duck if things go wrong. I can't let that happen."

He didn't have the authority to stop her, but she knew the determined look in his eyes wasn't about power. He wanted her safe. Touched, she couldn't argue with him, not about that. "All right," she said quietly, "I'll do it. Just don't expect me to be happy about it."

A small smile teased his mouth. "Your objection is duly noted. Now that we have that settled, I'll load the horses into the trailer and get the dogs."

* * *

Thirty minutes later they were on their way. With the horse trailer hitched to the back of the pickup and John's dogs, Buster and Lucy, riding in the back of the truck, they returned to the spot where they'd found the dead yearling. It was still where they'd left it, though something had gotten to it during the night. And overhead, the buzzards were already starting to circle.

John didn't give her a chance to even look at it. "Okay," he said as he backed the horses out of the trailer, "you take Dusty and I'll ride Midnight. When I give Buster and Lucy the signal, they're going to take off like a rocket, following the lion's scent. When we finally catch up with the damn thing, it'll probably run up a tree. I'll tell you right now that I'm going to shoot it as soon as I get a clear shot, so don't be upset."

"I won't," she promised as he helped her into the saddle, then placed a rifle in the holster strapped to her horse. "I know it has to be done." Eyeing the rifle warily, she frowned. "It's loaded, I presume?"

He nodded. "And the safety's off. Just remember... you have to pull the hammer back before you pull the trigger. Okay?"

"As I'll ever be," she said with a grimace. "Let's go."

Glancing at Buster and Lucy as he swung into the saddle of his own horse, he said, "You heard the lady. Let's go."

He didn't have to tell them twice. With a sharp bark of excitement, they jumped out of the pickup and went to work, tails wagging furiously. Within seconds, they'd found the mountain lion's scent. With a eerie bark that sent a cold shiver sliding down Elizabeth's spine, the dogs took off across the pasture without looking back.

"Here we go," John told her, and put his spurs to his horse.

Her heart slamming against her ribs, Elizabeth pressed her horse to keep up.

Chapter 8

An hour later, they followed the dogs into a rocky canyon high in the foothills of the mountains. Almost immediately, the canyon walls cut out the sunlight, casting them in deep, cold shadows. Suddenly chilled to the bone, Elizabeth pulled on her jacket, but the warmth of the fleece did nothing to calm the nerves jumping in her stomach as she warily eyed the dark cliffs that seemed to be closing in around them.

Thirty feet in front of her, John called back over his shoulder, "Are you doing all right back there?"

"I'll be better when this is over," she retorted. "I don't like the looks of this."

"It shouldn't be much longer. When the scent is old, it can take the dogs a while to pick it up, but we don't have that problem, thank God. Listen to them," he said as the dogs bayed in excitement. "He's moving fast and they're right on his tail."

The dogs were, in fact, so excited they could barely contain themselves. Through the trees, Elizabeth caught sight of them with their noses to the ground, their tails wagging furiously. They raced over the rocky ground, checking their pace only when they had to dart around trees and boulders that blocked their path.

And as they led them deeper and deeper into the canyon, Elizabeth's anxiety grew. The big cat had to know they were trailing it. What would it do when it realized it was trapped in the canyon? Would it try to run? Or stand and protect its territory?

Her heart slamming against her ribs, she spurred her horse to catch up with John. When had she fallen so far behind? "John? Wait..."

Suddenly, ahead of them in the trees, Buster screamed in pain...and went silent.

Elizabeth felt every ounce of blood drain from her face as Lucy barked fiercely. "Oh, God!"

"C'mon!" John growled, and spurred his horse into a gallop.

Elizabeth spurred her own horse and raced

through the trees on Dusty's back like she'd been doing it all her life. All she could hear was Lucy growling angrily and Buster's awful silence. *Please, dear God, don't let him be dead. Don't let him be dead. Please, dear God...*

Then suddenly, before she was ready for it, she broke through the trees just ten steps behind John. And there, twenty yards away, lay Buster in a bloody heap, with Lucy standing guard, the hair on the back of her neck standing on end as she glared at the thick trees that cloaked the end of the canyon and barked angrily.

"Oh, God, no!"

John brought Midnight to a stop in a cloud of dust right beside the fallen dog and jumped down to examine him. "He's still alive! But damn, he's bleeding like a stuck pig! I've got to stop the bleeding—"

Unzipping his jacket, he started to whip it off, only to freeze as the mountain lion suddenly appeared out of the trees directly in front of them. "Son of a bitch! My gun!"

Whirling, he started to reach for his gun, but his jacket was half off, binding his arms. Horrified, Elizabeth watched the big cat crouch. Totally ignoring Lucy, its golden eyes never left John as it prepared to spring.

Her blood turned to ice, freezing her in her tracks. The thunder of her heart loud in her ears, she must have eventually moved, but she didn't remember it. Suddenly the rifle was in her hands and she had no knowledge of removing it from its holster.

There was no time to think, no time to even take aim. She jerked the gun up, pulled back the hammer and pulled the trigger…just as the lion sprang.

Time ground to an abrupt halt. Over the thunder of her blood in her veins, she heard a woman scream, and only then realized that the horrified cry that echoed in her ears and up and down the canyon came from her own throat. *"No!"*

She should have moved, should have at least jumped to help John, but her feet suddenly felt like they were lodged in cement. Tears spilled into her eyes, making it impossible to see. Swearing, she wiped them impatiently away, only to gasp at the sight of the mountain lion lying dead less than three feet from where John had fallen backwards when the animal sprang.

"Oh, my God!" Hurriedly shoving the rifle back into the holster, she jumped off her mare and rushed to his side. "John? Are you all right? *John!*"

Struggling up, he swore roundly. "I'm fine," he growled, finally struggling free of his jacket, "thanks to you. That was a damn good shot."

"It was pure luck and you know it." Her heart still pounding, she cast a wary eye at the fallen cat as Lucy approached it cautiously. "Is he dead?"

"Oh, yeah. Buster's the one I'm worried about."

Grabbing his jacket, he hurried to the fallen dog. "We've got to get the bleeding stopped," he told her as she quickly dropped to her knees beside him, "then get him to the vet." Folding his jacket, he pressed it to the gash on Buster's chest. "Here. Hold this while I tie it in place."

Her eyes swimming with tears, she quickly did as he asked, then nearly lost it when Buster licked her hand. "It's all right, boy," she choked softly, stroking his ears with her free hand. "You're going to be fine. Isn't he?" she asked John, glancing up at him as he yanked off his belt to tie the makeshift bandage in place. "Tell me he's going to be all right."

"He's going to be all right," he said quietly. "If we get him to the vet in time."

Tears spilled over her lashes. "Oh, God."

"Do you think you can hand him to me once I'm mounted?" he asked her. "He's heavy."

"I can do it," she assured him, and carefully cradled the dog close when John handed him over. She staggered slightly under his dead weight, but there was no way she was going to drop him. Stepping over to Midnight as John stepped into the saddle, she struggled to hold the dog steady as she lifted him up to John. It wasn't easy. Her arms were shaking before she lifted the dog to shoulder level.

"What about the lion?" she asked as she jumped into her own saddle. "Shouldn't we take it with us or something?"

"We'll come back for it," he said shortly. "C'mon, Lucy," he called to the other dog. "Let's ride."

And with no other warning than that, he put the spurs to Midnight. A split second later Elizabeth raced to catch up.

The ride back to the spot where they'd left the truck and horse trailer was less than five miles away, but it seemed like a hundred. Elizabeth had never ridden so fast in her life and she was still fifty feet behind John. He and Midnight flew over the ground, barely kicking up dirt, and Lucy was right there with them. Marveling at the way that John held Buster so carefully and still managed to ride across rocky ground at the speed of sound, all she could do was try to keep up.

Then, before she realized how much ground they'd covered, they burst through the trees and there was the truck and horse trailer. Even as they brought the horses to a stop in a cloud of dust, John was throwing out orders. "Call Dr. Morrison on your cell so he'll be waiting when we get there. I don't remember his number—you'll have to get it from information. The keys are in my pocket. Start the truck while I cut the horses loose."

The keys are in my pocket. At any other time, her heart would have jumped in her throat at the thought of searching the pockets of his jeans while he was wearing them, but she didn't hesitate. Quickly dismounting, she hurried to his side and found the keys in his right pocket. Shoving them in her own pocket, she then took Buster so he could dismount. He took the dog back the second he was safely on the ground, and she sprinted for the truck as John followed more slowly, cradling Buster. She had the vehicle running and was already talking to Dr. Morrison before John carefully lowered the dog onto her lap. He only took time to jerk the saddles off the horses and unhook the horse trailer before signaling Lucy into the back of the truck. Seconds later they were racing for town.

Later, Elizabeth didn't remember much about the drive. All she saw was Buster, lying in her lap, his blood darkening the folded jacket pressed tight to his wound. Was his breathing more shallow than it had been earlier? Never taking her eyes from him, she asked, "How much farther?"

"Two miles," he said grimly, and hit the gas as they reached a straightaway.

Dr. Morrison was waiting, and even before John braked to a stop at the vet's office, he was there to take Buster and rush him inside to surgery. After that, there was nothing Elizabeth and John could do but wait…and wait. An hour passed, then another. It was enough to drive a sane person mad.

Then, just when she thought she couldn't stand the silence of her own worry another second, the swinging door that separated the lobby from the surgery area opened and Dr. Morrison joined them.

In his scrubs, the older man looked tired, but he was smiling. "He's one lucky dog," he told them as they both jumped to their feet. "It was touch and go for a while, but he's going to make it."

"Thank God," Elizabeth sighed, blinking back tears. "He lost so much blood."

"If it had taken you another ten minutes to get here, he might not have made it," he said soberly. "Needless to say, we'll be keeping him awhile. This isn't something he's going to recover from quickly. In fact, I doubt that he'll ever track again."

John had already come to the same conclusion. "That's okay. He's earned his chance to lay on the front porch and snooze."

"How did the lion fare?" the doctor asked. "Or did it get away when it took down Buster?"

For the first time in what seemed like a week, John laughed. "Not hardly. Elizabeth shot and killed it. And it's a damn good thing because it was just about to attack me. And she's only had one shooting lesson!"

Doctor Morrison grinned. "I guess it only takes one. So where's the lion? Did you leave it up in the mountains?"

John nodded. "We had to get Buster taken care of, but we're going back for it."

"Good. Bring it in and let me test it for rabies. I don't think anything's wrong—it sounds like the two of you got between it and its kill when you came to Buster's rescue—but I'd rather be safe than sorry."

"No problem," John assured him. "We're going back for it now."

Making it back to the canyon where they'd left the mountain lion turned out to be far easier than either of them had expected. With no scent to track, there was no need for the horses, so they took the pickup since it had four-wheel-drive and could traverse the rocky terrain of the canyon without any problem.

All too soon, they reached the clearing where they'd left the lion. It was exactly where they'd left it, and thankfully, no other animal had touched it.

"Do you think it might have had rabies?" she asked with a frown. "That might explain its behavior...."

"That's one reason I wanted to get the lion back to Dr. Morrison as quickly as possible," John said. "Rabies are transferable through an animal's food source. Anything that eats it will also get rabies."

Sitting between them in the cab of the truck, Lucy barked sharply and crowded John, wanting out, but John stopped her with a single word. "Stay! Good girl," he told her when she sat. "You're not going anywhere near that lion."

"What about the two of us touching it?" she asked John, suddenly horrified. "Do we have to worry about contracting the disease? Maybe we should call someone…."

"Who?"

"I don't know. Isn't there some kind of government agency that handles things like this? What about the sheriff?"

He snorted at that. "He's about as worthless as… Never mind. We don't need any help. We've got gloves and there's an old blanket behind the seat. Let's check him out."

Pulling on his gloves, he stepped out of the truck and over to the lion. "He's a big boy," he said, whistling softly as he squatted down to examine the body. "A hundred and eighty pounds or so. And damn old." Showing Elizabeth the animal's teeth when she cautiously moved closer, he said, "See how worn they are? That's why he went after the calves—they were an easy kill and he didn't have to work as hard for his dinner."

When she hesitated, lingering five feet away, he

grinned. "He's not going to hurt you. Come and take a look at him. He's your kill. What do you want to do with him after Dr. Morrison checks him out?"

"Do with him?" she asked, puzzled. "What do you mean?"

"You can stuff him."

"Oh, no!"

"Think about it," he teased. "You could put him in the entrance hall and have him mounted so he looks like he's about to attack. Then you attach a tape recorder to the front door so it sounds like a cat's snarling every time the door opens. You'll never have to worry about break-ins again."

"Or visitors, either," she said dryly.

"And you can eat him, of course, even if you do stuff him—if he doesn't have rabies."

"*Eat him?* Are you serious? What does mountain lion taste like?"

"Chicken."

For a minute, she thought he was serious. Then she saw the twinkle in his eyes. "It does not!"

"I had you going there for a minute, though, didn't I?" he chuckled. "Actually, it tastes a lot like pork—it's mainly white meat. So...what are you going to do? Stuff it, eat it, or both?"

How could she possibly answer that? "I'm going back to England in a couple of weeks," she reminded him. "I don't think I'm going to be able to get on the plane with a stuffed mountain lion."

"Probably not," he agreed with a grin. "But you still need to get it stuffed. My God, you only shot a gun once before in your life! And then you kill a lion without even taking aim. And in case you've forgotten, that damn lion was about to kill *me!*"

Her lips twitched. "So I should have it stuffed to remember you by?"

"Well...yeah. I mean, what's not to love?" When she just lifted a dark feminine brow at him, he laughed. "You're a hard woman, Elizabeth Wyatt. If you don't want to save the lion for me, think about the stories you'll be able to tell your grandchildren. If you have the lion stuffed and you can show it to them, how cool is that?"

Elizabeth almost smiled. Grandchildren weren't something she often thought about, but she had to admit—John had a point. Not even her great-grandfather Buck could beat her mountain lion story.

"All right," she agreed. "I'll have it stuffed and save the meat. But everything has to stay here until Priscilla graduates and she and I open our dress shop. In the meantime, as the ranch foreman, you get to not only take care of all the details, but also convince Buck and Rainey that a stuffed mountain lion is just what this family needs."

"No problem," he chuckled. "From what I've seen of Rainey, she won't even blink at the idea of a stuffed lion in the entry, and Buck is so crazy about her that he'll go along with just about anything she wants."

Elizabeth had to agree with him. She'd never seen her brother so happy. He adored Rainey, and the feeling was mutual. Envy tugged at her heart. Did they know how lucky they were? She'd thought she loved Spencer—when she discovered he'd cheated on her, she'd been devastated—but now, only weeks later, she barely remembered what he looked like. And when she closed her eyes and tried to remember his kiss, all she could think of was John.

Startled by the thought, she stiffened…and found her gaze locking with John's. Hot color burned her cheeks. Did he know she was thinking of him? His kiss? The way his mouth seduced hers? Did he know how she ached for him to do it again? How she longed for him in the middle of the night—

Suddenly realizing where her thoughts had wandered, she said thickly, "We need to go. Dr. Morrison is probably wondering where we are."

His gaze narrowing on hers, John didn't even hear her. He hadn't missed the color climbing in her cheeks. What was she thinking? His eyes searched hers, then, with a will of their own, dropped to her mouth. Damn, he wanted to kiss her! How long had it been? Hours? Days? It seemed like years.

So what if it does? Reason drawled in his head. *If you kiss her again, you're not going to be able to stop yourself from falling in love with her. Then what are you going to do when she goes back to England?*

"You're right," he said roughly, jerking his attention back to the matter at hand. "Let's get him in the back of the truck."

Forty minutes later they delivered the lion to the vet, then headed back to the Broken Arrow as the sun started to sink behind the mountains to the west. John would have liked nothing more than to just spend the rest of the evening taking it easy, but Elizabeth was awfully silent. He wasn't surprised. It had been a rough day. He wouldn't be surprised if she had nightmares tonight.

"Are you hungry?" he asked her as they approached the entrance to the ranch. "We can both change, then go back into town for dinner and a movie. It might take your mind off things."

"Actually, if you don't mind," she said quietly, "I'd rather just go sit in the hot springs at the Indian summer camp. I'm really sore from all the horseback riding and just want to soak for a while. But you can go to the movies, if you like," she assured him quickly. "I'll be fine by myself. The springs aren't that far from the house."

Even if he hadn't been worried about protecting her from whoever the hell was trying to drive her away from the ranch, did she really think he would leave her alone after they both could have been killed by that damn lion this afternoon? What if another lion was lurking in the dark somewhere, waiting to pounce the second she turned her back? She'd never know what hit her.

"No, I'll go with you to the springs," he said easily. "You need someone to stand guard. We don't know for sure that there aren't any more lions around."

"Oh, no! You don't need to do that. What are the odds of there being another lion around? I'll be—"

"Fine," he finished for her. "I know. And you're right—the odds of another lion being in this area are slim to none. But you're still not safe…which is why we agreed that you wouldn't go anywhere alone."

"But no one will even suspect I'll be there," she argued. "Especially after dark."

Far from convinced by her argument, he said, "How do you know that? Someone could have been watching us all day, following us. They might be out there in the dark right now, watching everything we do, waiting for a chance to get to you."

In the gathering darkness of twilight, she

blanched. "Are you serious? Or are you just trying to scare me?"

"Of course I'm serious. And if just talking about it scares you, how do you think you're going to feel if you're at the springs by yourself and someone comes up on you in the dark? The point is that these people, whoever they are, have already proven themselves to be pretty damn ruthless. All I'm asking is that you don't underestimate them. Don't think just because you don't see them that they're not there."

Just the thought of someone surprising her in the dark, miles from the house, turned her blood to ice. "Okay," she said huskily, "you made your point."

"Good," he retorted as he parked in front of the house and unlocked the front door for her. "I'll wait for you here. Don't forget to bring a robe. After sitting in the springs for any length of time, the night air feels really cold."

Twenty minutes later, when they reached the hot springs, Elizabeth only had to take one look at the place to know why the Native Americans had spent their summers there for hundreds of years before the white man ever set foot in North America. In the light of the full moon that had just cleared the tops of the trees to the east, the hot springs were beautiful. A soft breeze stirred the leaves of the trees, carrying whispers of the past, and all too easily, she could imagine the Indian teepees spread out in the moonlight. There would be music and laughter, cooking fires and horses, and children running everywhere.

Caught up in her musings, she'd completely forgotten John was at her side until he said gruffly, "It's got atmosphere, doesn't it?"

"And ghosts. Can't you feel them?"

Another man might have laughed and asked her if she was kidding, but he only nodded, his expression somber as he watched the white steam from the springs silently sway like a ghostly dancer in the glow of the moonbeams. "I've never seen a ghost, but if there is such a thing as spirits coming back to a place they loved, this is where you'd find them."

As they parked the Jeep and approached the springs on foot, the peacefulness of the place wrapped around them like a physical caress. Silence echoed in their ears, broken only by the soft gurgle of the water as it bubbled up out of the ground and spilled into a hot, deep pool that was surrounded by boulders worn smooth over the years by wind and rain and the countless feet of visitors who'd been drawn to the inviting warmth of the springs.

Every instinct John possessed told him to check out the area to make sure it was secure, then retreat to the trees at the far end of the springs so she could have her privacy. But damn, she didn't make it easy for him. Looking up at him, she smiled wistfully in the moonlight. "Sure you don't want to join me?"

There was nothing he wanted more, but resisting her was already next to impossible. If he got in that damn pool with her, he knew he wouldn't be responsible for his actions. "I didn't bring a suit."

A smart woman would have said, "Maybe next time, then." Instead, Elizabeth said, "Then I'll take mine off." And without waiting for him to say another word, she stepped over to the pool, found a place to lay her towel and robe, then began to undress.

Frustrated, mesmerized, he told himself not to look at her, but he was fighting a losing battle. "Dammit, Elizabeth! This isn't smart—"

For an answer, she unzipped her jeans and stepped out of them, leaving her standing before him in her bathing suit and a cover-up. The cover-up was the next to go, landing on her jeans with a nearly soundless whisper. Her eyes trained on his, she reached behind her for the hooks to her bikini top.

"I'm warning you," he growled. "Stop—"

Her gaze never leaving his, she peeled off her bathing suit top and dropped it onto her pile of clothes. A smart man would have told her about his past and the price his best friend had paid for his carelessness. But he was only human, and he only had so much willpower. With a groan, he jerked his T-shirt over his head and threw it on the ground. A split second later, he reached for the zipper of his jeans.

Her heart pounding, Elizabeth had all of five seconds to rethink what she was doing. There was, however, nothing to think about. The day had been a traumatic one, and whenever she closed her eyes, all she could see was the mountain lion as it crouched to spring. If she'd brought her rifle up five seconds later, if she'd *missed*…

Her stomach dropped at the thought. No! she told herself firmly. She wasn't going there, wasn't going to relive those moments over and over again. From now on, when she thought of today, she would think of the ranch's hot springs in the moonlight…and John walking naked into the pool.

Would she regret it later? He had a problem with the fact that she was his boss, but she wasn't asking the man to marry her. She just wanted to forget today, forget everything except how John made her feel when he kissed her. And what was wrong with that? She didn't want him to break her heart when she returned to London, but that didn't mean she wasn't attracted to him. He was driving her crazy. What would it hurt to give in to that attraction? Just once?

But as she sank down into the water and let the hot

water close around her shoulders, he didn't move to her side as she expected. Instead, he settled across from her in the small pool and stretched out his legs toward her. Under the water, his feet brushed hers.

In the moonlight, her eyes met his. Did he know what he did to her with just a touch? Could he hear the sudden thundering of her heart over the bubble of the hot springs? Did he know how badly she wanted him to take her in his arms and just kiss her?

So tell him, a voice in her head told her. *You've come this far. Don't stop now.*

"Why are you all the way over there?" she asked huskily. "You're not afraid of me, are you?"

His eyes were dark and mysterious in the moonlight. "What do you think?"

"What am I supposed to think?" she retorted. "You're not even within touching distance."

"Sure I am," he replied, and stroked her foot under the water, tickling her toes with this.

Teasingly, she pulled her feet back six inches. "You were saying?"

"You don't play fair," he growled, but he didn't move closer.

Disappointed, she frowned. "Was it something I said?"

"No," he replied. "It was something I didn't. There's something you need to know."

Chapter 9

"That accident I told you about…the one when I was in the Navy?"

"Yes. What about it?"

"I dropped a rifle," he said coldly. "It discharged when it hit the ground and my best friend was shot in the head."

She blanched. "Oh, John, I'm so sorry!" she gasped, shocked. "But it was an accident—"

"I was trained to handle weapons, Elizabeth, not drop them. Because I was careless, Mark died. He was twenty-three years old, for God's sake."

There was no emotion in his voice, nothing but

coldness in his eyes. Fighting sudden tears, Elizabeth could only imagine the guilt he must have carried around all these years. His best friend! Dear God, how had he stood it?

"I'm so sorry," she said quietly. "That must have been incredibly difficult for you."

"It was the worst thing that ever happened to me. I should have been the one who died—"

"No! Don't say that!"

"So I got out of the Navy and spent the next six years trying to drink myself to death," he continued as if she hadn't spoken. "My wife left me. I lost everything."

"Including the ranch your parents left you," she guessed, suddenly realizing why he wasn't working his own operation. "Oh, John, you must have gone through hell."

Leaning back against the rocks that formed the edge of the pool, he stared back into the past. "I thought losing my wife was the worst, that nothing again could ever hurt that badly, but she wasn't gone two hours when I learned that the bank was repossessing the ranch because I couldn't pay the home equity loan I'd taken out on the property to pay the taxes. I'd grown up there—my parents are buried there. And I lost it all because I was a drunk."

Her heart aching for him, she studied him in the moonlight. "Is that when you quit drinking?"

He nodded. "That was the worse day of my life…and one of the best things that could have happened to me. It was a wake-up call," he said simply. "I realized that I was going to have to deal with my alcoholism if I was ever going to get my life back. So I joined AA and went to therapy to help me deal with Mark's death. I've been sober for the past three years."

"Doing that all by yourself must have been incredibly difficult."

"Don't make me out to be a hero," he warned her. "I'm not even close."

Elizabeth disagreed. He'd fought out of the depths of a despair that she couldn't even imagine, and he'd done it alone. Just thinking about how he must have felt the day he lost everything—his wife, his home, everything he cared about—brought the sting of tears to her eyes. How had he stood it?

"Don't be so quick to cut yourself down," she told him. "After everything that happened to you, a lot of people would have just given up. You didn't."

"I suppose that's one way of looking at it," he retorted. "Obviously, you're one of those people who sees the glass as half-full instead of half-empty."

Grinning, she shrugged. "It depends on what the glass is full of. If it's lemonade, then it's half-full. If it's prune juice, that's another matter all together."

"You won't get an argument out of me," he said

with a reluctant smile. "So, Ms. Wyatt, now that I've told you my secret, what's yours?"

"You know mine. The man I was in love with cheated on me when he was in Germany for a soccer tournament." Her mouth twisted in a smile that had little humor. "So much for happily every after. It's a myth, you know. There's no such thing. The government made it up."

"Oh, really? And who told you that?"

"My boyfriend's new girlfriend."

"That would do it," he agreed. "Look at it this way—you were the lucky one. He's probably already moved on to someone else."

"Oh, he has," she said. "My sister Priscilla e-mailed the latest headlines to me. Now he's with a redhead in Ireland. The man's a total loser."

"I dated a woman once like that…"

He told her about the first woman he lost his heart to, the same woman who dumped him for a friend, and she found herself telling him about Mitch, the art student who'd filled her head with romance when she was seventeen, taken her virginity, then walked away without a backward glance. He'd never called her again. She'd cried for weeks.

"I thought I'd never trust a man again," she admitted huskily. "Then I met Victor, then Clarence, then Spencer—"

"And stepped right back on the merry-go-round," he finished for her with a crooked smile. "I did the same thing with Susan, then Becca..."

"And Mary Jo and Allison and Denise," she teased. "You probably had women beating down your door to get to you."

His brown eyes dancing with amusement, he shrugged. "Maybe. Maybe not. I was shy."

"Yeah, right. And I'm the Queen Mother."

"Okay, Your Highness. It's getting late. We should be getting back to the house. Have you soaked the stiffness out of your muscles yet?"

She stretched under the water and sighed in relief as her limbs moved easily. "Oh, that's much better. Now if I can just manage to stand up. My legs feel like they're made of jelly."

She staggered slightly as she tried to push to her feet, and he was there in a heartbeat to catch her before she could fall. Suddenly they were whisper close, both naked except for her wet bikini panties, their hearts pounding and eyes locked on each other in the moonlight.

Move!

Somewhere in the far reaches of her mind, her common sense barked out orders, but her body wasn't listening. *She* wasn't listening. Not when she couldn't take her gaze off his eyes, his mouth. She'd never wanted to kiss a man so badly in her life. With a murmur of need, she leaned closer, then closer still, and brushed his mouth with hers. Once, twice, featherlight. Then his arms closed around her, gently drawing her against him, skin to skin, and she melted against him with a moan that seemed to come from the depths of her being.

"You're driving me crazy," he groaned. "Are you going to kiss me or not?"

"Maybe," she teased. "I'm still thinking about it."

"Then think about this," he growled, and covered her mouth with his.

His kiss was hot and hungry and far too short. Aching, needing more, she kissed him back, only to have him pull away and set her from him. "John!"

Reaching for one of the towels she'd brought with her and set on a rock next to the pool, he unfolded it and slowly slid it over her shoulders and down her arms, wiping away the moisture with a gentle, persistent tenderness that stole the breath right out of her lungs. With every swipe of the towel against her breasts, her thighs, the curve of her hip, her bones melted one by one.

Shuddering, aching, she reached for the other towel she'd brought and pulled it slowly over his shoulders and back, then down to his hips, teasing him as he had teased her. And with every groan she pulled from him, the need that burned between them grew hotter.

With a murmur that was her name, he stepped back, but only long enough to spread her robe out on the rocky ledge of the pool. Then he was reaching for her in the moonlight, pulling her down with him, into his arms as the rising steam from the springs swirled around them, touching their bare skin, silently caressing them.

Her bikini panties disappeared, but Elizabeth hardly noticed. Every sense she had was focused on John—the scent of him, the feel of his hands roaming over her, the hard, hot heat of him covering her, warming her from the inside out. Everywhere he touched, she burned. Then his mouth followed his hands, kissing every inch of her, and with a flick of his tongue, he had her arching in startled pleasure, crying his name in the night.

"John!"

"Do you know how beautiful you are?" he rasped, kissing the curve of her waist, her breast, the side of her neck. "You're driving me crazy."

"You're pretty good at doing that yourself."

He chuckled, only to groan as her hands trailed over him in slow motion. "Tease."

"You haven't seen anything yet," she promised, giving him a slow, seductive smile. And with no more warning than that, she set about the business of destroying what was left of his control.

Up until then, he would have sworn that he was the one in charge of their lovemaking, but he'd obviously been wrong. With a gentle push of her hand, she rolled him onto his back. Then she was rising over him, moving over him with gentle hands and mouth, teasing, seducing, setting him on fire with a tenderness that nearly destroyed him.

With a touch, a kiss, the stroke of her tongue, she pushed him over the edge. Suddenly, what was left of his control snapped, and with a groan that seemed to be ripped from the heart of him, he swept her under him. The springs, the night, the world itself, receded, and there was only the two of them as his eyes met hers in the moonlight. With a murmur that was her name, he kissed her, and then she was lifting her hips to his. He surged into her, and as they both found themselves caught up in a dance that was as old as time, there was no turning back. There was only the two of them, mindlessly racing toward an end that neither of them could see. Then, just when they thought they knew what to expect, they shattered with a force that seemed to blow the stars right out of the night sky.

Elizabeth couldn't remember the last time she'd been so happy. It couldn't last—she knew that—but it didn't matter. She never before experienced anything even close to what she and John had shared, and she knew she was going to spend whatever time she had left in the States with him.

The logical part of her brain warned her she was making a mistake. Having an intimate relationship with him now would only cause problems later, when she visited the ranch in the future. Years from now, she would only have to see him, look into his eyes, to know what could have been…if she hadn't inherited the ranch and become his boss, if he hadn't made a mistake in the Navy all those years ago that he was still punishing himself for. If. So many ifs. He was going to steal her heart. She knew that as surely as her eyes were blue. It didn't matter. Nothing mattered except that she wanted him in a way that she'd never wanted a man in her life.

Last night was…incredible. There was no way other way to describe it. After they'd made love, they'd bathed in the springs again, then returned to the house and slept the rest of the night in each other's arms. She'd made breakfast for them because she couldn't bear for their time together to end. She was making dinner for the two of them tonight for the same reason.

As she headed into town, she smiled at the sight of the sheriff's deputy following a discreet two hundred yards behind her. When she told John she was going to the grocery store, he'd been in the middle of changing the oil in the tractor. He was dirty and greasy, and she couldn't blame him for not wanting to drop everything so he could run her into town. But he'd refused to let her go alone. So she'd called the sheriff's office and asked if one of the deputies could escort her to town and back. If it hadn't been a slow day, the deputy she spoke to probably would have turned her down. Instead, he pulled up before the house fifteen minutes later and assured John he wouldn't let her out of his sight.

When she reached the only grocery store in Willow Bend, however, he didn't, thankfully, follow her inside. The last thing she needed was a babysitter when she was buying milk and eggs! Grabbing a cart, she pulled out her list and headed for the produce section first.

"Get out of my way, bitch."

In the process of picking through the tomatoes for a ripe one, she looked up in surprise...and found a middle-aged woman with fading red hair glaring at her with hostile eyes. Stunned, she said, "I beg your pardon?"

"You're not welcome here. If you've got any brains, you'll leave while you still can."

"Excuse me? I don't know who you are, ma'am, and don't care to. But just for the record, I'm not going anywhere. If *you* had any brains, you and your kind would know that." Deliberately turning her back on the other woman, she returned to her tomatoes.

For a moment she half expected the woman to pick up a tomato and smash her in the back of the head with it. Her heart pounding, she waited, but the woman obviously thought better of confronting her further. With a sniff of disdain, she walked away.

Relieved, Elizabeth didn't know if she wanted to laugh or follow the woman and tell her exactly what she thought of her. How dare she! What was wrong with the people of Willow Bend? Did they really think they could terrorize her and her brother and sisters into leaving? They obviously didn't know the British side of the Wyatts!

The fire of battle burning in her eye, she returned to her shopping, but she didn't get very far before her cart was slammed into by a cowboy with a case of light beer in his basket. He took one look at her and brushed past her, knocking her into a standing display of canned tomatoes. Not surprisingly, when one can was knocked out of place, the others went flying.

Catching herself before she fell to the ground, Elizabeth heard snickers but refused to be embarrassed. *Let them laugh,* she thought coolly as she bent down to collect the cans that had rolled into the middle of the walkway. They wouldn't be laughing when the year was up and she and her family were still at the Broken Arrow.

"Here, let me help you with that. I don't know what got into Tommy Guthrie. I've never seen him act so ugly before."

Surprised that anyone would offer to help her, Elizabeth looked up to find one of the store clerks hurrying forward to help her. "Since I don't know Mr. Guthrie, I can only assume that he's the jackass that nearly knocked me out of my shoes."

Plump and smiling, her dyed blonde hair teased into a frizz, the other woman grinned. "That would be Tommy." Holding out her hand, she said, "Hi. I'm Lily Cunningham. You must be Elizabeth Wyatt."

Elizabeth knew she should have been wary—she had enemies all over town and didn't even know who they were—but there was something about Lily's bright smile and direct green eyes that she trusted immediately. "Yes, I am," she replied, shaking her hand. "How did you know?"

"The British accent," she replied promptly. "It's wonderful. And, of course, everyone knows that your sisters went back to England, so you must be Elizabeth."

Her smile fading, she added, "I'm sorry everyone's being so mean to you."

"It's more than that. Whoever is trying to drive us away has committed everything from harassment to destruction of property. They even tried to kill Rainey! And they're not going to get away with it," she vowed. "If we find out who's doing this, we will press charges."

"I don't blame you," Lily said as she helped her pick up the last of the tomato cans. "I'd do the same thing. The way I look at it, Hilda wouldn't have left the four of you the ranch if she didn't want you to have it. And you're the last of the Wyatts, for heaven's sake! The Broken Arrow wouldn't be the same place without a Wyatt living there."

Thankful everyone in town wasn't against her, Elizabeth smiled. "You don't know how much I appreciate that. I was beginning to think everyone in town hated my guts."

"Not everyone," Lily assured her. "In fact, most people in Willow Bend are pretty decent. Any town's going to have a few bad apples. We just seem to have more than most."

"Oh, that's reassuring," she said with a chuckle. "I feel better already. Thanks."

The sales clerk smiled, but there was no doubting her sincerity when she said, "Just remember you're not alone. I know it may not seem like it, but a lot of people around here are pulling for you and your brother and sisters."

Elizabeth appreciated that, but later, as she stood in line to pay, she could still feel the hostility of the other shoppers. Were any of them responsible for the attacks on the ranch? she wondered. Lately, she'd mentioned her suspicion to the deputy who'd escorted her to town, but he didn't seem too concerned. And that was the problem. Surely, someone in town had to know who was trying to drive them away, she reasoned as she headed home with the deputy following two hundred yards behind her. If they did, however, they weren't talking. Not a single person had stepped forward or even made an anonymous call to the sheriff to identify their attackers.

Why? she wondered as she took her eyes from the road to find another station on the radio. If there were decent people in Willow Bend—and she had to believe Lily wasn't the only one—why hadn't someone stepped forward? Why—

Distracted, she never saw the bullet that slammed into the windshield, shattering it.

"This is Deputy Reynolds, Mr. Cassidy. I'm at the hospital with Miss Wyatt. She wanted me to call you to tell you that someone shot out the windshield of the Jeep."

"*What?* Is she all right?"

"She's a little upset right now..."

"What do you mean 'upset'? Upset how? Is she hurt?"

"Actually, she's cussing like a sailor," the deputy said dryly. "I thought I'd heard it all, but the lady's got a real way with words."

If he hadn't been so worried, John would have laughed. Instead he growled, "I'll be right there."

Slamming down the phone, he only took time to wipe the oil from his hands before grabbing the keys and running for the pickup. Fifteen minutes later he was running for the emergency room entrance before he'd hardly braked to a stop. In his head, all he could see was Elizabeth, cut and bloody and disfigured for life....

The emergency room doors opened then, and there stood Elizabeth, toe to toe with Sherm Clark, the sheriff. She did have a cut on her hand that was covered by a small bandage, but it obviously wasn't bothering her. Livid, she glared at Sherm, not the least bit intimidated by the fact that he towered over her by at least a foot and outweighed her by 125 pounds.

"What kind of sheriff are you?" she demanded. "Are you even listening to yourself?"

"All I said was—"

"I heard what you said!"

"What's going on here?" John said sharply as he stepped forward. "Elizabeth, are you all right?"

"I was until the sheriff showed up," she retorted,

scowling at the older man with disdain. "Tell John what you told me. I dare you."

"You don't have to act as if I suggested something obscene," he told her coldly. "All I said was that it might not be in your best interest to be in Colorado right now. And if you don't believe me, then maybe you need to take another look at your Jeep. It has no windshield, in case you've forgotten."

"I haven't forgotten anything. In case you haven't noticed, I'm still wearing the damn glass!"

"There's no need to swear..."

John saw fire flare in her eyes and quickly stepped between them. Just that quickly, he found his arms full of an angry, sputtering woman. "Calm down, Elizabeth. He's just trying to keep you safe—"

"Safe!" she echoed, outraged. "He's not trying to keep me safe—he's trying to get rid of me!"

"You're damn straight—" the older man snapped "—so nothing will happen to you!"

"If you'd do your job, you won't have to worry about anything happening to me," she retorted, glaring at him over John's shoulder as he held her at bay. "Why is this so difficult for you to understand?"

"Elizabeth—"

Ignoring his warning, she said softly, "Just so there's no misunderstanding, Sheriff, listen carefully. I'm not going anywhere. Okay? Spread the word, tell whoever you want to, put it in the newspaper. I'm staying until Buck returns from his honeymoon, and I or one of my sisters will be back whenever he needs one of us to stay. We'll do whatever we have to, but one thing we won't do is lose the ranch. Remember that."

Not giving him a chance to say another word, she turned her attention back to John as all the fight seemed to go out of her. "Can we go home now? I'd really like to leave."

She didn't have to tell him twice. "Of course. Let's get you out of here." And putting his arm around her shoulders, he walked her over to the truck. Suddenly noticing she didn't have anything with her, he frowned. "Where's your purse?"

"Deputy Reynolds has it. He put the groceries in his patrol car, then called a wrecker for the Jeep." Sighing as he helped her into the pickup, she laid her head back against the headrest and closed her eyes. "I don't know what's wrong with me," she said with a yawn. "I can't keep my eyes open."

"Don't worry about it," he told her, squeezing her hand. "It's been a rough day. Just close your eyes and rest." Suddenly spying the deputy standing by his patrol car, he said, "I need to get your things from Deputy Reynolds. I'll be right back."

Still pale and already half-asleep, she nodded imperceptibly, and never even opened her eyes. Studying her, imagining how scared she must have been when the windshield exploded right in front of her, John didn't want to think about what would have happened if the shooter had aimed more to the right.

Suddenly furious, he strode across the parking lot to where the deputy waited and growled, "What the hell happened? How could some jackass shoot out her windshield when you were right there?"

"I wish to God I knew," he retorted, his expression grim. "I was two hundred yards behind her, everything was fine, and suddenly all hell broke loose. Right before her windshield shattered, I saw a flash at the edge of the trees in the distance. By the time I called for backup and an ambulance, whoever was in the trees was long gone."

"What about footprints? Or tire prints? There had to be some kind of sign that someone had been there."

"If there was, I couldn't find it," he retorted. "Granted, it's a gray day and the light was starting to fade, but the ground was rocky and what dirt there was was covered in pine needles."

Disgusted, John swore roundly. "I can't believe the bastard's audacity! He shoots out her windshield, and there's a deputy right behind her. And he's going to get away with it!"

"We're doing everything we can, Mr. Cassidy, but

when we don't have much to work with, there's not a heck of a lot we can do."

"Well, you're not doing enough," he retorted. "And neither am I. I thought she'd be safe with an escort."

"So did I," the deputy said honestly. "Unfortunately, if someone wants to get to her badly enough and is willing to risk anything, it won't matter if she's surrounded by every law enforcement officer in Colorado—the jackass will find a way. If I were you, I wouldn't let her out of my sight."

John was left with no choice but to agree with him. "Thanks for your help," he said, offering his hand. "If you hadn't been there, she could have been in big trouble."

"If you need any help, just give me a call," Reynolds told him. "Oh, yeah, don't forget Elizabeth's purse and groceries. I'll help you carry it to your truck."

As good as his word, he helped carry everything over to the pickup and was just putting the last sack in the vehicle when he got another call. With a wave, he was off, as was the sheriff, with sirens blaring.

Climbing into the pickup, John finally had a moment alone with Elizabeth. Turning to her in the growing darkness, he said quietly, "We need to talk."

She stiffened. "If you think you're going to talk me into going back to England, I can tell you right now we're going to fight. I'm not leaving, damn it!"

"I won't let you risk your life," he retorted. "If that means I have to throw you over my shoulder and carry you off the ranch, then by God, I'll do it. And don't even think about reminding me that you're my boss," he added when her chin came up and her eyes narrowed dangerously. "I don't give a damn. I don't need your permission to protect you."

She didn't doubt for a minute that he meant every word—but so did she. "I'm not leaving the ranch, John," she said quietly. "So if you want to protect me, you're going to have to do it on the Broken Arrow."

"How the hell do you expect me to do that—" he began, only to kick himself as a thought came to him. "Damn! Why didn't I think of it sooner? There's an old hunting cabin up in the mountains on the far west side of the ranch. I'm sure Hilda never used it, so it probably hasn't been used in years. I doubt that anyone even remembers it exists. We could hide out there for months and no one would have a clue where we are. What do you think?"

"But if no one knows we're there, won't people assume I've left? We could lose the ranch."

She had a point. "Wait—there's a video camera in Buck's office," he told her. "If we film you at the cabin with today's paper—"

"That's all the proof I need to prove I was on the ranch," she said, delighted. "It's perfect!"

Chapter 10

They loaded the pickup with clothes and blankets and what seemed like enough food for an army, then headed for the mountains. The nightmare of the shooting forgotten, Elizabeth couldn't remember the last time she'd been so excited. She'd read all the family journals and autobiographies about the ranch, just as Buck had, and she knew all the stories about bear hunting and Indians and living in a small cabin in the wilds of Colorado during the 1800s. And when she'd come to the States for Buck's wedding, one of the things she'd promised herself to see before she returned home was the mountains—and cabin—where the ranch first started.

When John pulled up before the cabin, however, it looked nothing like what she'd expected. The small one-room cabin wasn't falling down, but to say it needed repairs was a gross understatement. There was no indoor plumbing or electricity, the roof was missing a dozen or more shingles, and the floor of the small porch had a hole in it the size of a picnic basket. Dead leaves and pine needles had collected in nooks and crannies on the porch and windowsills, and cobwebs clung to the rafters. The front door was wide-open, and it was painfully obvious that no one but an occasional raccoon or bear had used the cabin in years.

Watching the shock register on her face, John said, "Don't blame me. Your ancestors built the place. People were tough in those days."

Her chin came up at that. "Are you saying I'm a wimp?"

His lips twitched. "Who, me? Never!"

"I'll have you know I'm just as tough as my ancestors," she retorted. "If you don't believe me, you just watch." And grabbing a broom and the cleaning supplies they'd brought with them, she stepped into the cabin.

Grinning, John said, "Call if you need me. I'm going to fix the roof, then chop some wood."

Elizabeth hardly heard him. Stepping into the doorway, she stopped, wrinkling her nose in distaste at the sight of the mess animals had made in the cabin. There was a nest of twigs and leaves in the corner, the bones of a dead animal in another, and a smell she didn't want to identify. Tying a bandanna around her mouth and nose, she went to work sweeping out all evidence of rodent infestation. Then she pulled out the pine-scented antibacterial cleaner they'd brought to disinfect the cabin.

Hours passed. She heard John hammering overhead as he repaired the holes in the roof, then he turned his attention to chopping wood, but she hardly noticed. As she cleaned out the fireplace, her eyes drifted to the queen-size blow-up bed John carried into the cabin for her as soon as she finished cleaning. She took one look at it and felt her heart start to pound.

"Uh, wh-where—" Suddenly realizing she was stuttering, she stiffened. When had she given the man the power to make her stutter?

"I should have asked you if wanted one bed or two," he said with a slight smile, "but it gets cold up here at night. We'll need to share each other's body heat."

"It's May," she pointed out. "How cold can it get?"

"Midthirties," he said with a shrug. "Possibly colder. The elevation's a lot higher up here than it is at the homestead. Have you noticed the snow under the trees?"

She hadn't—she'd been too busy cleaning the cabin. "Snow, huh?" she quipped. "Well then, I guess I need to set the bed as close to the fireplace as possible and make sure we have plenty of blankets."

Amusement glinting in his eyes, he turned and walked out.

Stacking the last of the firewood he'd cut, John found himself grinning at the memory of Elizabeth's face when she'd realized there was only one bed. He'd expected her to balk when she saw the cabin—what woman wouldn't?—but he should have known better. Over the course of the past few weeks, she'd thrown herself into learning how to run the ranch and she hadn't complained once. She wasn't one of those women who was afraid to get her hands dirty, and that never failed to surprise him. She was beautiful and feminine and sophisticated—even when she had dirt on her nose.

And she didn't disappoint him when it came time to cook dinner. She didn't even blink when he announced that during their stay at the cabin, all meals would be cooked on the campfire. "We've got all the pots and pans we need?"

He nodded. "It's all in the wooden box by the campfire. Have you ever used a Dutch oven?"

Already going through a box of cooking supplies,

she looked up in surprise, interest sparking in her eyes. "No. Did you bring one?"

"I found it in the kitchen pantry. It looked pretty old. There's no telling how long it's been in the family."

Digging quickly through the box, she found it at the bottom and pulled it out, grinning like a little girl who'd just discovered that Santa had brought her just what she'd secretly wished for for Christmas. "Oh, my God! This is so cool! I've read about these. You set it in coals, then put more coals on the lid and it cooks just like an oven!"

"That's the idea," he laughed. "I remember my grandmother making biscuits in one when I was a kid. Nothing cooked in a regular oven ever tasted as good."

Thrilled, Elizabeth felt as if she'd stepped back in time as she started dinner. They'd have grilled chicken, baked potatoes and biscuits. She'd never made biscuits, only scones, but they were similar enough that she didn't expect any problems. And a salad, she decided. John had brought boxes of groceries from the house—surely there had to be ingredients for a salad dressing somewhere. As happy as a kid in a candy shop, she started digging through the boxes.

Darkness came early, closing in on the small clearing where the cabin sat, and as they sat by the campfire and ate dinner, they seemed like the only two people in the world. Overhead, the stars sparkled like diamonds, and as John watched Elizabeth relax in the glow of the firelight, he couldn't take his eyes off her.

"Dinner was amazing," he said quietly.

She smiled softly in the firelight. "Thank you. I was pretty pleased with it myself."

"In case I haven't mentioned it before, you're doing a good job around here. You've taken on the duties of the ranch without a word of complaint, and I can't think of many women I could say that about. Your Wyatt ancestors would be proud of you."

Color spilled into her cheeks. "Thank you. Before I came to the States, I researched everything I could about the American West just so I'd have some kind of idea of what to expect. But nothing really detailed day to day life, especially for the women. It must have been incredibly difficult. Can you imagine living up here in the dead of winter? People must have been amazingly tough."

"They were," he agreed. "When I was a kid, I remember my great-grandfather talking about his great-grandfather, who cleared his land and built a log cabin with no one but his wife to help him. There were no power tools, no crane to lift the heavy log rafters, no crew to do the heavy work. And the closest town was nearly a hundred miles away. How the two of them did that by themselves just boggles the mind."

Stretching his feet out to the fire, he stared at the flames, trying to imagine how a man and a woman could accomplish such a task and build something that was still standing today. "They were tough, all right. My great-great-grandmother delivered seven children in that log cabin without a doctor or midwife or drugs. And she and my great-great-grandfather lived into their eighties. They were amazing, and the Wyatts were, too, if the stories Buck told me are anything to go by.

"Not that I have to tell you that," he added quickly. "Like you said, you've read the journals."

When Elizabeth didn't respond, he glanced to his right where she sat with a blanket wrapped around her shoulders and her feet stretched out to the fire. Her head was slumped forward slightly, her eyes closed. Even from a distance it was obvious that she wasn't resting her eyes. Her breathing was slow and shallow, and John could have sworn she was snoring.

Emotions tugging at his heart, he couldn't take his eyes off her. It had been a long day, and she'd worked nonstop cleaning the cabin, then cooking. She had to be exhausted.

Rising to his feet, he stepped into the cabin and checked the fire he'd laid earlier. It had burned down and was in need of more wood. Adding a few more logs to the fire, he pulled back the covers on the bed, then went back outside to bank the coals of the campfire. Only then did he turn to Elizabeth.

She was right where he'd left her, curled up in one of the lawn chairs he'd brought for the two of them. The edge of her blanket was trailing on the ground, but she never noticed when he stepped over to her and wrapped the blanket closer around her. Sound asleep, she only sighed and dropped her head on his shoulder when he picked her up.

At the feel of her breath against his neck, he swallowed a silent groan. How in the world was he going to resist this woman who was so totally different from what he'd thought she was? She fit in his arms as if she'd been made just for him, and every time he touched her, kissed her, he found it more and more difficult to let her go. Making love to her once was a mistake. Doing it twice would, he knew, make it become a habit. If he was smart, he would run, not walk, away from her. She was going to rip his heart right out of his chest and take it with her when she went back to England, but there wasn't a damn thing he could do about it. The only chance he'd had of walking away from her was the day he'd met her. If he hadn't been able to do it then—when he didn't even know her—how could he now?

Cradling her close, he carried her into the cabin and carefully laid her on the bed. Only taking time to shut the cabin door, he sank down onto the side of the bed and pulled off her boots and his. As they hit the floor and he slipped under the covers with her, clothes and all, Elizabeth rolled toward the middle of the bed, as the mattress gave due to his heavier weight. Just that quickly, she was snug against him.

Soft. Why, he wondered with a groan, did she have to be so soft? Sound asleep, she snuggled against him, driving him crazy, and with a will of their own, his hands found the buttons to her blouse and slipped them free, one by one. When the backs of his fingers brushed her breasts and she moaned, whatever was left of his common sense went up in smoke. Giving in to the need clawing at him, he kissed her, gently drawing her from sleep, until her hands were roaming over him, stroking, rubbing, slowly driving him out of his mind.

He must have called her name, though he had no memory of it, because suddenly, she was pushing him to his back and rising above him in the light of the dancing flames in the fireplace. "Say it again," she rasped softly. "You call my name that same way in my dreams."

He couldn't have denied her if his next breath had been his last. "Elizabeth. Sweetheart." For a moment he couldn't manage anything else but a groan. Then, when he could string a sentence together, he said thickly, "Witch. Do you have any idea what you're doing to me?"

Her smile turned seductive in the firelight. "I believe it's the same thing you do to me. If you'd rather I didn't, though, I can stop—"

"Don't you dare," he growled, and pulled her back down to him and covered her mouth with his. Teasing her with fingers that were as quick and seductive as hers, he unhooked her bra, then reached for the snap of her jeans. Before she could do anything but gasp, his fingers dipped inside.

Surprised, she only had time to cry out in delight before he was taking her to the outside boundary of control. Then before either of them could guess how close to the edge she was, he took her over. She was still shuddering when he pulled the rest of her clothes from her and surged into her. When she shattered again, he did, too. By the time he finally floated back to earth, he couldn't remember his own name. He didn't care.

She was falling in love with him.

Over the course of the next few days, Elizabeth fought the truth with every fiber of her being, but every time she found herself watching him and felt her heart turn over, she knew she was fighting a losing battle. He was everything she'd ever wanted in a man. Smart, hardworking, caring, honest. And she didn't see how they could possibly have a future together.

His pride was the problem, of course. She didn't care if he worked for the family, but he did. She didn't know what to do about it. She couldn't change her family circumstances anymore than he could. And if he loved her—and he hadn't even hinted at his feelings—she liked to think that he wouldn't let the fact that he worked for the Wyatts get in the way of the two of them being together. She couldn't, however, be sure that that's how he felt, and it was tearing her apart. She could live in a one-room cabin with him for the rest of her life and not utter a single word of complaint.

Suddenly realizing where her thoughts had wandered, she almost laughed. Her family would never believe she was the same Elizabeth who hadn't wanted to come to the States because she wouldn't be able to get a decent cup of tea. She'd changed. She was in love, and it was wonderful.

"Okay," John said as he helped her finish the last of the breakfast dishes in plastic dishpans they'd brought from the house, "how about going for a hike this morning? I have something I want to show you."

"What?"

"Oh, no," he said with a laugh. "If you want to know, you have to come with me."

Her eyes sparkling with interest, she studied him consideringly. "Okay, lead the way."

"First, we're going to need a few things," he told her, and quickly put together a sack lunch and filled their canteens with water. Grabbing his binoculars, the camera and his rifle, he grinned. "We're all set. Let's go."

It was a beautiful May morning, cool and crisp, without a cloud in the sky. Leaving behind the clearing where the cabin was, they struck out through the trees, heading farther up into the mountains. Within minutes, they found themselves surrounded by the quiet stillness of the forest. Far above their heads, the wind whispered secrets in the tops of the pines, but all they heard was the crunch of their boots on the pine needles underfoot.

"So where are we going?" Elizabeth asked, lengthening her stride to keep up with him. "Since you brought water and lunch, it must be quite a hike."

"Maybe," he quipped. "Maybe not."

Torn between frustration and amusement, she huffed, "Okay, be that way. I'll figure it out." Studying him as they came to a stop to appreciate the view, she frowned at the binoculars he'd slung around his neck. "Is this it?" she asked, turning to look out over the mountains that stretched to the horizon. "You wanted me to see the mountains?"

"Nope," he chuckled. "But the view's pretty spectacular, isn't it? Wanna take a picture? Better take it now. By the time we come back this way, it'll probably be dark."

"Dark!" she repeated, startled. "Are we going that far?"

Grinning, he only shrugged. "Maybe—"

"Maybe not," she finished for him, rolling her eyes. "Okay. I get it. You're not going to tell me. Lead on."

With a grin, he took her hand and pulled her after him.

They reached the crest of the first line of hills and started down the other side. Her eyes on John's back, all her senses attuned to the warmth of his fingers wrapped around hers, she couldn't have said later how far they walked or where. Then, just when she was beginning to wonder if they were going to hike all the way to Denver, he stopped so suddenly that she bumped into him.

"Sorry," she said, only to glance past him when he half turned toward her and stepped back, allowing her to see the small stream that wandered through the mountain meadow in front of them. "Oh, how pretty. Wait...what's that? Oh, my God! Is that a—"

"Bald eagle," he finished for her quietly. "I didn't know if you'd seen one before." Handing her the binoculars, he nodded to the east. "Look down the river about a half mile," he whispered, "in the tall aspen on the cliff. See that pile of brush in the limbs on the right? That's a nest."

Scanning the river in the distance with the binoculars, she gasped, "My God! This is incredible! Why didn't you tell me about this?"

"I just did," he chuckled. "That's why we're here. Look, there's an eagle diving for a fish right now."

Her heart pounding, she shoved the binoculars at him, but only to grab her camera. Laughing, he pulled her down beside him on the nearest rock so she could eagle watch as long as her heart desired.

The sun was on its downhill slide when they finally left the valley where the eagles nested and started the hike back to the cabin. This time, John stayed beside her on the trail, and when he took her hand, the day couldn't have been more perfect.

"Did I forget to say thank you?" she said huskily. "I can't remember ever enjoying a day so much."

His fingers tightened around hers. "I thought you would like it. I still remember the first time I saw an eagle."

"How old were you?"

"Five—I think," he chuckled. "I went fishing with my father, and we were floating down the Snake River in Wyoming in our rubber boat. We were miles from anywhere, and suddenly, I looked up and there was an eagle sitting on a dead limb in the highest pine on the river. We floated right under it."

"Are you kidding? That must have been incredible."

"I'll never forget it," he said simply. "It was right after dawn, and the sunlight was sparkling like diamonds on the river. I wasn't looking for eagles—I don't even know why I looked up. Then suddenly there was this magnificent creature, looking right at me. To this day, I've never seen anything so beautiful in my life."

"I know what you mean," she said huskily. "I didn't expect—"

When she hesitated, unable to find words, his eyes, warm with good humor, cut to hers. "Gets to you, doesn't it?" he said with a smile.

She couldn't deny it. "I can see why my ancestors fell in love with Colorado. Can you imagine seeing it back in the eighteen hundreds? It must have been—"

Suddenly breaking off in midsentence, she frowned, searching the trees in front of them. "Do you smell something? It smells like—"

"Smoke," John finished for her, stopping in his tracks with a scowl. "Where the hell would smoke be coming from?"

Elizabeth didn't want to say the words, but there was no avoiding them. "A forest fire? Is it possible?"

"It's always possible," he replied, "but not very likely on a day like today. The weather's been great. There's been no storms, no lightning. Unless someone got careless with a campfire or something, which isn't likely. This is all part of the Broken Arrow. There are no campers out here. There's no one here except us…that we know of."

Elizabeth paled at his words. "The cabin—"

Swearing, John started to run. "Come on!"

They were a mile from the cabin and had a long run up a steep ridge and down the other side. By the time they reached the edge of the clearing where the cabin was, they were both panting from the exertion and Elizabeth had a stitch in her side that burned like fire. They never noticed. Their eyes on the cabin, all they could see was the black smoke pouring out of the windows and the flames licking at the roof.

"Oh, my God!"

"Quick. Start filling buckets and throwing them on the fire," John shouted as he grabbed a shovel. "I'll throw snow on it while you hit it with water."

The cabin didn't have indoor plumbing—the only water came from an old-fashioned hand pump attached to the well fifty feet away. If the cabin hadn't been burning right before her eyes, Elizabeth would have realized that she and John had an impossible task in front of them. But her heart was in her throat, her blood pounding, and all she could think was that the cabin had been built by hand by her ancestors. Once it was gone, it was gone forever. Desperate to save it, she grabbed the bucket John thrust at her and ran for the well.

Frantic, she pumped the icy water into the bucket, then sprinted for the cabin, spilling nearly half of it as she went. She never felt the cold sting of it, not when the heat from the flames scorched her cheeks.

Hurry! The word echoed in her head like a scream, but when she lifted the bucket and tossed what was left of its contents onto the fire, she couldn't take time to even see if it made a dent in the flames. Whirling, she ran back to the pump.

She didn't notice how many buckets she filled and poured on the fire—they all blurred together. Her hands ached from working the pump, from carrying the heavy bucket to the cabin, but she couldn't stop. Not when the flames were licking at the roof.

Beside her, John wildly shoveled snow onto the fire. Sweat dripped from him, and she knew he had to be exhausted, just as she was, but he never checked his desperate pace. Only, nothing either of them did seemed to do any good. The fire continued to rage unchecked.

A sob rose in Elizabeth's throat. "Please, dear God, please…"

What was she praying for? A miracle? Divine intervention? Inspiration?

At first she didn't notice. All she could feel was the heat from the fire against her face as she threw another bucket of water on the blaze. Then, as she ran back to the pump, her feet suddenly slipped out from under her on the damp grass. The next thing she knew, she was flat on her back, staring up at the darkening gray sky above.

"Elizabeth!"

"I'm all right," she assured him breathlessly, struggling to sit up. "I slipped."

"Did you hurt yourself? Break something?" Scowling when she didn't answer, he growled, "Dammit, Elizabeth, what's wrong with you? Say something!"

Stunned, she lifted fingers that weren't quite steady to his wet cheek. "It's raining."

Chapter 11

Within seconds, the light drizzle became a steady, drenching downpour. Still on the ground, Elizabeth didn't know if she wanted to laugh or cry. The cabin was saved…such as it was. One section of the roof was badly damaged—the rain was, no doubt, pouring into the cabin—but she knew they couldn't complain. If the rain had held off another thirty minutes, the cabin would have been a total loss.

"It's going to be okay," John told her as he helped her up and wrapped his arms around her. "We can fix the roof, sweetheart. Trust me, between the two of us, we can have it as good as new in no time."

Shaking from the coolness of the rain and the aftermath of the near disaster, not to mention exhaustion, she buried her face against his chest, just barely fighting off tears. "It's my fault," she choked. "This is all my fault."

His arms tightened around her, pulling her close. "How do you figure that?"

"I must not have banked the coals in the campfire very well," she sniffed. "The wind must have picked up a spark and carried it to the roof."

It was a logical explanation, and the only one that made sense…until John said quietly, "Smell the air, honey. What do you smell?"

A frown wrinkled her brow as she pulled back slightly to blink up at him in the rain. "Smell? I smell smoke, of course." The last of the flames had gone out, but the blackened remains were still smoldering. "And rain. Why? What do you smell?"

But even as she asked, she caught the faint scent of an odor that was common enough, but didn't belong there in the pure mountain air of the mountains. Her eyes wide, she stiffened. "Gasoline."

His expression grim, he nodded. Someone had found them.

Her heart in her throat, Elizabeth looked around wildly, but there was nothing to see but the silent pines that surrounded them on all sides. Was someone out there watching them? Chilled, she hugged herself and tried to convince herself that she was just being paranoid, but she couldn't shake the sinister feeling that seemed to seep out of the shadow of the trees and trail icy fingers down her spine.

"Do you think they're still here?"

Her nearly soundless question didn't carry past his ears. John grabbed his rifle, then handed her hers, his eyes already searching the trees. "Shoot anything that moves," he murmured.

There'd been a time in the not too distant past when she'd have sworn that, regardless of how comfortable she became with guns, she would never be capable of shooting an animal, let alone a human. But as she stood back-to-back with John and closely examined the darker shadows of the surrounding woods, she knew she was not only capable of pulling the trigger, but that she would if whoever was terrorizing her made the mistake of stepping out of the trees.

Their uninvited visitor didn't, however, show his face. The woods were eerily silent—even the birds were quiet.

Confused, Elizabeth never took her eyes from the trees as she said quietly, "How could anyone find us? We're miles from the house. No one knows we're here. How would they even know where to look?"

John had been wondering the same thing. He'd

been damn careful to make sure they weren't followed, so how the hell had the bastard found them? He'd have sworn that no one could have possibly seen them. How could he have missed someone tracking them? Where had he messed up?

An image played in his mind, teasing him, haunting. Yesterday, when he and Elizabeth sat down to lunch, it was a beautiful summer day. There wasn't a cloud in the sky, and there'd been only a slight breeze. As they'd sat by the campfire, the smoke from the fire had lifted straight into the air…pointing like a finger to the small private plane that had flown directly over the cabin as they ate.

"Damn!"

"You've thought of something."

His expression hard, he reminded her of the plane that neither of them had paid much attention to yesterday. "If whoever was piloting that plane was looking for us, the smoke from the campfire told him right where we are."

"So he hiked in to kill us?"

"If he'd wanted to kill us, all he had to do was set the cabin on fire last night while we were sleeping," he retorted bluntly. "No, he doesn't want us dead. He just wants you gone. If he burns you out, it just might be enough to scare you into going back to England."

"Then they're wasting their time," she retorted

coldly. "When are these people going to get it? They're not going to scare me into leaving."

"I think it's time to call Buck."

"No! Dammit, John—"

"The threats are escalating," he cut in. "Whoever started the fire may not intend to kill you, but they're not above scaring the hell out of you. And accidents happen. You could get seriously hurt."

"Buck will be home in two days. I really only need one more night. We won't invalidate our claim to the ranch if I leave tomorrow and Buck comes home the following day. We just can't be absent from the ranch two nights in a row."

He shouldn't have listened to her—she was in danger and that was all that mattered. He should have gotten her out of there right then and there and taken her to Colorado Springs or Aspen, anywhere other than Willow Bend or the Broken Arrow Ranch. It was the only logical thing to do. Buck would come home the second he heard about the fire, she could go back to England where she would be safe, and he wouldn't have to worry about her anymore.

If she'd been anyone else but who she was, there wasn't a doubt in his mind what he would have done. He would have insisted she get out of Dodge. But his gut knotted just at the thought of her leaving. He'd known she had to leave eventually, of course, but he'd thought they had more time. He'd hoped she might stay another week or two after Buck and Rainey returned from their honeymoon, but that obviously wasn't going to happen. She was leaving, and for her own safety, she had to get out of there. Tonight was all they had left.

"If you're going to stay," he said grimly, "then we need to make damn sure that whoever started the fire is long gone. Then we need to fix the roof. C'mon, let's check the woods."

It didn't take them long to discover that whoever had torched the cabin was no idiot. He'd left no evidence behind, not even a burnt match.

"So much for that," John told her, disquieted.

Shivering, Elizabeth hugged herself and once again checked the surrounding trees. "Do you think someone's still out there?"

John followed her gaze to the silent, always silent trees. Just as before, nothing moved. "I wish to hell I knew," he finally said honestly. "If I was trying to just scare someone, not hurt them, I wouldn't stick around to get caught."

"And whoever started the fire had to know we weren't here," she pointed out. "If he really wanted to hurt me, he would have waited until we returned from our hike."

"Exactly," he agreed. "Unless he was grossly incompetent, burning the cabin was nothing more than a scare tactic on his part."

"So you think he's gone?"

"There's no way to know for sure, but he certainly appears to be. The question is...what do we do about tonight? The cabin's scorched, and whoever torched it is probably watching the house to see if you come back there. I suggest we stay here."

"But there's a hole in the roof, and everything smells like smoke!"

"I've got time before dark to patch the roof," he assured her. "As for the smoke smell, there's not much we can do about that. If the weather was nice, we could sleep outside, but judging from the look of the sky, we're not done with the rain. So what do you want to do? Sleep in the smoky cabin or take your chances and go back to the homestead and hope someone doesn't torch that, too. It's your call."

She didn't even have to think about it—she wasn't putting the homestead at risk. "Let's stay here."

"Then we'd better get busy before the rain starts up again. It doesn't look like we've got much time."

Within minutes, John was up on the roof, inspecting the damage done by the fire. It wasn't, thankfully, as bad as he'd first thought, but with Elizabeth's help, they still had a couple of hours of work ahead of them. Quickly measuring the hole in the roof and estimating how much wood he would need, he went to work cutting rough shingles.

"I'll come back later and fix it right," he assured Elizabeth as she helped him carry the shingles up the ladder to the roof, "but this will at least get us through the night."

"While you're finishing this, I'm going to clean up inside and see if I can get rid of some of the smoke smell," she said with a grimace as she carefully made her way across the roof toward the ladder. "Though I don't know what we're going to sleep on. The fire melted the blow-up mattress and all the covers are covered in soot—"

Her eyes on where she was stepping, she couldn't see the intruder who stood in the trees a hundred yards away. Or the rifle that was aimed at her and John. Until, with no warning, a shot rang out.

"What the—"

Alarmed, she whirled, her eyes wide…just in time to see John stagger backward and fall off the roof. Horrified, she screamed. "No!"

She practically threw herself down the ladder and rushed to John's side. Her heart slamming against her ribs, she prayed frantically. "Please, God! Please don't let him be dead! Please…"

He was white as a sheet, but he groaned when she

touched him. "John? Thank God!" Tears flooding her eyes, she wiped them impatiently away as she saw the red seeping through the wound in his shoulder. "Don't move," she told him when his eyes fluttered open. "I've got to stop the bleeding—"

A second shot rang out from the trees to the right, kicking up dirt just inches from where she knelt next to him.

"Bastard!" she screamed, flinching. "Leave us alone!"

"The rifle," John gasped, wincing as he struggled without success to sit up.

"Where—"

"I left it by the cabin door."

She saw it then, propped in the open doorway, and there was no time to think as their attacker fired off another shot. She quickly grabbed the rifle and fired five shots into the trees.

Almost immediately she heard someone grunt in pain, but she didn't have time to worry about how badly she'd wounded their attacker. Her only concern was John.

"C'mon," she said, moving to help him to his feet. "I've got to get you inside before they start shooting again."

Groaning as he regained his feet, he leaned against her heavily. "How do you know there's more than one?"

"I don't, but we're not taking any chances," she said grimly. "We don't know how many people are out there. Until we do, we've got to assume it's an army."

He couldn't argue, not when he was bleeding like a stuck pig. He pressed a hand to his shoulder as Elizabeth helped him inside the cabin, but it didn't help. Blood seeped through his fingers and dripped onto the floor. If she hadn't held him up, he would have fallen flat on his face.

Worried sick, she eased him down to the floor. "We've got to get the bleeding stopped. You're white as a ghost."

"I'm all right," he said tightly. "It's just a flesh wound."

"And I'm the queen," she retorted. "Look at you. There's blood all over you and you're weak as a kitten. Hold still."

With no warning, she jerked off her T-shirt and folded it into a compress that she pressed to the wound. Then she grabbed a knife.

John had seen her naked more than once; he'd made love to her and kissed every inch of her body. But he'd never thought she was more beautiful than when she sat there before him in just her jeans and a bra and cut her shirt into strips to secure the bandage in place at his shoulder.

"I've got to get you to the hospital."

His shoulder on fire from the bullet, he couldn't take his eyes off her. "If you take me to the hospital dressed like that, I'll bleed to death before anyone notices I'm alive," he said with a crooked, painful grin. "I can see through the lace of your bra."

Her lips twitched. "Shut up."

"Yes, ma'am. Anything you say, ma'am, as long as I can keep looking at you. Did I tell you how beautiful you are?"

If he hadn't been in so much pain, he would have laughed when she sniffed and said, "Would you behave yourself? I'm trying to save your life, in case you hadn't noticed."

"I'll try to remember that," he chuckled, only to groan when she tied the bandage more firmly into place.

She paled. "I'm sorry! It has to be tight."

"I know," he said hoarsely, squeezing her hand. "I'm not complaining. Do what you have to do, sweetheart. Without you, I'd be in serious trouble right now."

"John, you're bleeding like a blooming pig, and whoever shot you is probably still out there somewhere in the trees, waiting to finish you off, then go after me. If that's not serious trouble, I don't know what is."

He grinned weakly. "You may have a point. So what's the plan, boss lady? I presume you have one."

She nodded, sobering. "I have to get you to a

hospital, but since we don't know if there's anyone else out there, waiting for a chance to finish us both off, we're going to have to wait until dark to make our move. I'll sneak you out to the truck, and we'll drive out of here before anyone's the wiser."

As far as plans went, it couldn't have been simpler…or more dangerous. John didn't have the heart to tell her that the second she started the car and the truck headlights came on, they would be sitting ducks. Or that once it was dark, whoever wanted them dead would also use the darkness to their advantage. Like it or not, any way you looked at it, the two of them were toast.

He couldn't, however, take hope away from her. At the moment, it was all they had. "Okay," he said, squeezing her hand, "we'll wait for dark."

Twilight was less than thirty minutes away, full darkness at least an hour after that. The bandage covering John's wound was dark with his blood, and even though the bleeding had slowed significantly, she hadn't missed the fact that he was growing weaker. He still held her hand, but his grip wasn't as strong as it had been, and that scared the hell out of her. How was she going to get him to the truck if she couldn't even get him up on his feet?

Worried, all her attention focused on him, she didn't

notice when the evening turned to night. Sitting next to John on the floor, her eyes straining to watch his every breath, she suddenly realized that the last of the daylight had disappeared into the night, and she didn't even know how long she'd been sitting there in the dark.

Her heart pounding, she swallowed, forcing moisture into her suddenly dry mouth. It was time.

"John?"

For a moment, she thought he was unconscious. He didn't respond to her nearly soundless whisper, and fear burned like an inferno in her gut. Then he murmured in the darkness, "Help me up."

Quietly, she reached for him in the dark and helped him sit up. Outside, a cold rain began to fall, and within seconds, found its way through the hole in the cabin roof. Before Elizabeth could tug John to his feet, the gentle rain became a deluge.

Suddenly everything seemed a hundred times worse. Tears stung her eyes, and her shoulders slumped in defeat. Now what was she supposed to do? It wouldn't take long for the clearing the cabin sat in to become a quagmire in this kind of weather. Even if she could get John to the truck without him slipping in the mud, how was she going to drive the truck down the mountain? There was no road, only narrow dirt paths on the side of the mountain that could, no doubt, become treacherous in a pounding rain.

"It's going to be all right," John told her gruffly in the darkness, hugging her close in spite of the pain she knew had to be burning his right shoulder and arm. "If anyone's still out there, they're not going to sit out in this kind of weather long. They know I'm hurt and there's no way in hell you're going to be able to get me out of here. If they've got any brains in their head, they'll head for home and come back in the morning."

"I'm not worried about them," she choked, burying her face against his neck. "What if you fall in the mud before you reach the truck and I can't get you up? What if we get stuck? I've never used four-wheel drive before. What if there's a mud slide—"

John looked her squarely in the eye. "What if the brakes go out or we have a flat or the Martians fly in under the low cloud cover and take over the world? What'll we do?"

Lost in her panic attack, it was a long moment before his words registered. When they did, she pulled back to give him an arch look in the darkness. "I beg your pardon? Did you say 'Martians'?"

His teeth flashed in a grin. "Did you say 'mud slide'?"

Struggling not to smile, she said, "If you're trying to imply that worrying about a mud slide is as ridiculous as looking for Martians on radar, then you obviously don't know what you're talking about."

Far from offended, he only chuckled. "Did I ever tell you that I love it when you go queenie on me?"

"You'd better stop, mister. I'm in no mood for your teasing."

"There you go again. Where'd you leave your crown, sweetheart?"

She tried not to laugh and failed miserably. "Wretched man. You better be glad I'm not the queen. I'd just call for your head after I saved your hide, and then what would you do?"

"Really?" he chuckled. "So now *you're* going to save me?"

"That's right." Sobering, she tightened her arm around his waist. "Ready?"

He nodded grimly. "On the count of three."

Soundlessly moving to the front door of the cabin, they stood in the open doorway and studied the truck, which was parked twenty feet away, at the far end of the cabin. The driver's side was closest to the cabin, and they'd already decided that they would both get in the vehicle on that side. Now it was just a matter of carrying out the plan.

Bracing herself for the cold splash of the rain and the hot scream of an assassin's bullet, she could barely manage to whisper the words. "One. Two. *Three!*"

The first step was the hardest. Fear clutching her heart with steely talons, she hardly winced as the rain slapped her in the face. Instead, she found herself holding her breath, listening for the scream of a bullet, waiting for it to rip through her skin and tear the life out of her….

The shot they both expected, however, never came. But that did nothing to ease the tension that set the air in the cab of the truck humming. Quickly helping John slide across the bench seat to the passenger side, she fumbled with the key twice before she was finally able to jam it into the ignition. With a flick of her wrist, she started the motor, threw the transmission into Drive, and hit the gas.

The trip out of the mountains and into town was one of the most harrowing of her life. Rain beat down on the truck like bullets, but she never checked her pace. Slipping and sliding over the muddy track that at times seemed to disappear beneath the truck tires, she fought with the steering wheel until her knuckles were white, dodging trees and boulders and somehow, just barely managed to stay on the road.

Beside her, John never said a word, but Elizabeth knew he had to be hurting as she jerked the wheel just seconds before she would have sent them careening over the edge of a cliff that suddenly appeared out of nowhere in the darkness. “I'm sorry,” she gasped as she brought the truck back under control.

"You're doing great," he said hoarsely. "Don't worry about me."

But she did. His shoulder had to be bleeding again. If he hadn't had his seat belt on, she would have thrown him to the floorboard. Racing downhill through the trees like it was some kind of obstacle coarse from Hell, they were both tossed against doors and each other, and more than once, she heard him groan.

Just the thought of hurting him sickened her, but she couldn't take a chance and slow down. Not when whoever shot John could still be out there, watching, waiting…following. That scared the hell out of her. She couldn't call the police, an ambulance, couldn't let anyone, even the authorities, know where they were and what was going on because whoever she called for help might be in on the conspiracy to bring down the Wyatts.

"I'm taking you to the hospital," she told him as they finally reached the main road. "Hold on." Leaving the ranch behind, she flattened the accelerator to the floorboard and just dared anyone who might be following them to keep up.

"Tomorrow morning, I'll drive out to the cabin and check things out," Deputy Reynolds told John and Elizabeth an hour later, after John's shoulder had been cleaned and bandaged. "But I've got to be honest with you both—I don't expect to find anything. This jackass has been one step ahead of us every step of the way. I can't see him screwing up now."

John had to agree. "Do what you can. Just know that we will, too."

"You won't get an argument out of me," the deputy replied. "You have every right to defend yourself. If the circumstances were different, I'd tell you to get out of town for a while, but I understand why you can't do that. Just be careful."

They'd been nothing but careful…and ended up in the emergency room. Resigned to the fact that they were on their own, Elizabeth waited until she and John were back in the privacy of the truck before she announced, "I called Buck while the doctor was stitching you up."

Surprised, he said, "I thought you didn't want to do that."

"I didn't. He should be able to leave the ranch in my care and not have to worry about losing the place while he's gone. Especially when he's on his honeymoon! But I'm not going to let you get shot or killed and stand around with my hands in my pockets and do nothing. So I called Buck and my sisters. This affects all of us, and they all needed to know what's going on."

"So what did he say? He's coming home?"

She nodded. "He should be here tomorrow."

Tomorrow. That was all they had. Her heart stopped at the thought.

"I think we need to go to a hotel for tonight."

Still caught up in the pain of knowing she would be leaving him, she suddenly blinked at his words. "No! We can't."

"Why the hell not?"

"Because it's too risky. If we're not at the ranch tonight and whoever shot you finds a way to keep us away tomorrow night, too, the ranch is lost forever."

"But Buck will be here tomorrow," he reminded her.

"Maybe. Maybe not," she said with a shrug. "Think about it, John. Whoever's after the ranch seems to know every move we make. How do you know they aren't tailing Buck and Rainey, too? Then the second Buck and Rainey start home, suddenly, they're hit by a hit-and-run driver. Their car is totaled, and it's impossible for them to make it home tomorrow. Normally, that would be no big deal. But I've already been away from the ranch for one night. All anyone has to do is find a way to keep me away from the Broken Arrow tomorrow night, and the unnamed heir can walk right in and claim the place."

John knew she was right, but his gut clenched just at the thought of taking her back to the homestead. The house was too big, too hard to defend, too vulnerable. But what choice did they have?

"All right," he sighed. "We'll go back to the ranch. But we're not staying in the homestead. We'll go to my cabin."

Chapter 12

When Buck and Rainey pulled into the driveway at two o'clock the following afternoon, John had never been so glad to see anyone in his entire life. "I'm sorry you had to cut your honeymoon short," he said, carefully offering his right hand for a brief shake, "but Elizabeth did the right thing when she called you. I can't protect her anymore. In fact, she's the one protecting me. She stayed awake all night, guarding the door to my cabin with a shotgun."

Buck's eyebrows climbed at that. "Are we talking about Elizabeth, my sister? The same one who gets hysterical when she sees a lizard in the garden and cringes at the thought of swatting a fly with a rolled-up newspaper? That Elizabeth?"

Far from offended, Elizabeth just grinned. "That's right, big brother. You'd be amazed at what I learned to do while you were gone, thanks to John. I can even cut cattle."

"Sounds like we're not the only ones who had fun while we were gone," Rainey said with a chuckle as she stepped forward to give her sister-in-law a hug. "Good. At least that makes up some for the rest of the garbage."

"I'm sorry I had to call you," Elizabeth said, sobering. "But I didn't know what else to do. When the attacks first started, I never thought it would turn so ugly. I kept remembering all the awful things that David Saenz did to the two of you. But he's dead."

"I was hoping that with David's death, the worst of it was over," Buck told her. "You should have called me and told me what was going on. Rainey and I would have come home immediately."

"Which is exactly why I didn't call you," she replied. "It was your honeymoon. I couldn't do that to you."

"And it wasn't that bad at the beginning," John added. "First, it was just threatening notes and cut fences and crap like that. Then someone shot the windshield out on the Jeep when Elizabeth was driving home from town. And she had a deputy following right behind her."

"What?"

"I wasn't hurt," she assured them. "It was just a scare tactic."

"That's when we decided to move to the cabin," John said grimly. "It seemed like the perfect place to hide out until you two returned from your honeymoon. It was miles from anything and no one could possibly know we were there. Then someone set the cabin on fire while we were eagle watching."

"Oh, my God!" Rainey gasped. "Thank God you weren't there!"

"It was a warning," Buck told her. "'We know where you are—you can't hide from us. So leave while you can. Next time, you may not be so lucky.'"

"And that's what we should have done," Elizabeth said. "Instead, we tried to repair the cabin after the rain put the fire out. That's when John was shot, and I realized then that whoever's after the ranch would do anything to get it. With John hurt, I needed reinforcements."

"What she needs," John said, "is to go back to England immediately. As soon as she packs her bags, I'm taking her to the airport."

Stunned, Elizabeth gasped, "The hell you are!"

She might as well have been talking to a wall. His

mouth compressed in a flat line, he retorted, "I'm not arguing with you about this. You're leaving, and that's all there is to it."

Elizabeth liked to think she was a reasonable woman who didn't lose her temper easily. But at his words, something in her just snapped. Did he really think he could lay down the law to her and she was just going to fall into line like some kind of obedient, weak-willed female who didn't have a brain in her head?

"No, I'm not leaving," she retorted. "Do you really think I would go off and leave you when you're hurt? What kind of woman do you think I am?"

"It's not safe here—"

"So what does that have to do with anything? I can't just fly off to London and leave you and Buck and Rainey to face the danger alone." Tears welled in her eyes at the thought, and that only irritated her more. Dammit, she would not cry! "In case you haven't noticed, I'm in love with you. I'm not going anywhere. If you don't like it, then too damn bad!"

Not giving him a chance to say a word, she stormed into the house and slammed the door behind her, leaving behind a stunned silence that echoed like a scream.

For what seemed like an eternity, no one said a word. Then Buck cleared his throat. "Well, it looks like quite a lot happened while we were gone." Lifting a brow at John, he grinned. "So what are you standing around here for? Are you really going to let her say something like that, then just walk out? Go after her, man."

John was still reeling from Elizabeth's announcement. She loved him? He had never been so frustrated in his life. "You don't understand. It's not that simple. She's my boss, dammit!"

"Apparently, she's a heck of a lot more than that," Rainey pointed out with a smile. "She's in love with you."

"And you're in love with her," Buck said, studying him with shrewd eyes that missed little. "Don't deny it. It's written all over your face."

His back to the wall, he growled, "So what if it is? It doesn't matter. I'm all wrong for her. You know that. I haven't held anything back from you. You know my past, Buck. I killed a man!"

Suddenly realizing what he'd blurted out in front of Rainey, he said, "I'm sorry, Rainey. I hate for you to hear this, but you might as well know so you'll understand..."

"I know," she said quietly.

"Rainey and I have no secrets from each other," Buck told him gruffly. "I told her everything. She believes like I do—it was just an unfortunate accident."

"I messed up," he insisted. "My best friend died because I screwed up."

"You're human, John," Rainey told him, "and accidents happen. You can't continue to punish yourself because of an accident you couldn't have possibly anticipated."

"I dropped my weapon. That's not allowed."

"Why did you drop it? What happened?"

He hated to go there, but the images were just as clear as they had been ten years ago. "I was teaching marksmanship in basic training, and two recruits started fighting. Mark was trying to break up the fight and shoved one of the men back. He tripped and fell into me. I dropped my weapon, it discharged, and shot Mark right in the heart. He was dead before he hit the ground."

"But that wasn't your fault! How could you be responsible when a recruit was pushed into you?"

"I shouldn't have dropped my weapon."

"You wouldn't have if someone hadn't slammed into you," Rainey pointed out. "Did Mark know you had a gun?"

"Yes, but—"

"No buts," she said quickly, cutting him off. "Mark knew you had a gun and shoved the guy right at you—"

"But he couldn't have known the recruit was going to trip and fall into me."

"Then how could *you* have? Why were *you* the one who was responsible?"

"Because I was in charge."

"But other SEALs were involved, SEALs who were, supposedly, trained the same way you were. SEALs," she added, "who should have anticipated the accident and known better than to start a fight during weapons training, but didn't."

"Out of all the people who were present that day, no one had a clue that someone was about to die, yet you blame yourself for not preventing the accident. How could you when no one else did?"

"Because..."

When he hesitated, obviously struggling for an answer, Rainey ached for him. "You're not psychic, John," she said quietly. "I'm sure you were a fantastic SEAL, but you couldn't possibly know everything. No one could. Which is why an innocent man died and no one could do anything to stop it. No one's to blame—it would have happened whether you'd been there or not. Let me ask you this—if the situation had been reversed and you had died instead of your friend, would he have blamed himself for the accident? Or would he have realized that some things are inevitable and only fate can determine the outcome?"

His eyes searching hers, he felt as if she'd just hit

him over the head with a hammer. He'd been carrying around the guilt of Mark's death for the past ten years, and it had nearly ruined his life. He'd lost everything—his wife, the ranch that had been in his family for decades, the future he'd taken for granted. And not once in all those years had he asked himself if his guilt was reasonable. He'd just assumed because someone—his best friend—had died that he had to be responsible.

"Quit beating yourself up, man," Buck said gruffly. "You did everything you could for your friend and it wasn't enough. He wouldn't expect you to punish yourself the rest of your life for something you had no control over. Let go of it and move on."

"That doesn't change the fact that Elizabeth's my boss," he pointed out grimly, "and I'm not the kind of man you would have ever wanted for your sister. Admit it. You would have never hired me if you'd thought Elizabeth was going to fall in love with me. I'm not exactly brother-in-law material."

"I don't know why the hell you would stay that," Buck retorted. "You were a Navy SEAL, for God's sake! You know how to protect her from anything short of an alien invasion, you're hardworking, and you've got more honor than just about any man I know. What more could I want for one of my sisters?"

When he just looked at Buck, stunned, Rainey

grinned. "Now that you've got that settled, there's only one thing left to discuss. Do you love her?"

"Well, of course I love her! It's been driving me crazy. *She's* been driving me crazy. I kept telling myself that she was my boss, that she was going back to England, and I was a fool to even think about getting involved with her, but none of that seemed to matter."

"I know how it is," Buck said dryly, slipping an arm around Rainey's waist to pull her close. "So why are you standing around here talking to us? Go after her and tell her how you feel."

For all of two seconds he hesitated. Then he grabbed Rainey for a quick hug, shook hands with Buck and rushed into the house.

Her heart felt as if it was being ripped out of her chest, but Elizabeth was determined not to cry. The minute she ran into the house, she escaped to her bedroom, but it didn't take long for her to realize that she was going to find little comfort there. It was too empty, too lonely.

Swallowing a sob, she stepped to the window and, for a moment, considered escaping outside, where she could cry in peace and grieve for a love that she was afraid was going to be over before it had hardly begun. Then her eyes drifted to the barn in the distance, and the foreman's cabin, which sat fifty yards beyond that.

John's cabin. If she lived to be a hundred, she would never forget her last night there. Waiting for dawn, she'd sat next to John's bed while he slept, her shotgun loaded and ready in case anyone came through the door after them. And no place had ever felt more like home.

Unable to resist the emotions that pulled at her, squeezing her heart, she decided to head for the cabin. John wouldn't be there, she assured herself. He would be in the office with Buck, discussing everything that happened over the course of the last month. He'd never know she'd even been there.

Hurrying down the back stairs that led to the kitchen, she was almost running by the time she hit the back door. Tears were streaming down her cheeks, but she didn't care. There was no one to see as she finally reached the front porch of the cabin and dropped down into the old rocker there.

She was looking for peace as she stared out at the mountains in the distance, and but what she found was the knowledge that she couldn't leave. Even if John never loved her, she couldn't leave. It was too late for that. The ranch had become her home, and she belonged there in a way she never had in London. She was staying.

But what about John? How will you stand it?

Wincing at the whispers in her mind, she hugged herself as she rocked. He had to love her.

Didn't he realize that she didn't care what his position was on the ranch? Who gave a rat's ass who he worked for? She loved him. Nothing else mattered if he loved her, too. Somehow, some way, she had to make him understand that. Because if she couldn't, they were doomed. Just the thought of that broke her heart.

Caught up in her thoughts, she didn't realize that she was no longer alone until John quietly stepped up onto the porch. She took one look at the determined set of his jaw and stiffened. "Don't mess with me, John," she warned him. "I love you. If you have a problem with me being part owner of the ranch, then we need to talk about it and find a way to work it out."

"I agree."

She had a head of steam up and she wasn't letting him get in the way of what she had to say. "I have never treated you like an employee—"

At his arch look, she said, "Okay, I may have thrown it at you a time or two when we first met because you were ordering me around, but what else was I supposed to do? Say 'yes, sir,' and salute? I don't think so."

His lips twitched. "I can't see you doing that, ever," he said with a chuckle. "You've got too much spunk for that. That's one of the things I love most about you."

"I can't help who I am any more than you can—" His words suddenly registered, stopping her in her tracks. "What did you say?"

"I said you had too much spunk to salute me—or anyone else, for that matter. That's one of the things I love about you."

Stunned, she just looked at him. "You *love* me?"

"It seems like I've been fighting it from the moment I met you," he admitted huskily.

If she hadn't already been sitting down, her knees would have given out completely. Confused, she frowned. "I don't understand. If you love me, then why are you sending me away?"

"Because you deserve the best," he retorted, "and I'm not it."

"That's not true!"

"I'm a recovering alcoholic, sweetheart," he said quietly. "You can't deny that."

Tears stung her eyes. "But that doesn't make you a bad person. You have your drinking under control. How long's it been since you had a drink? Three years? Five?"

"Six," he replied. "But every day is a battle."

"I know that," she agreed. "But it's a battle you're winning. So what's the problem?"

"All it takes is for me to slip once, and I could start drinking all over again. You don't need that in your life."

"That's not going to happen."

"You don't know that."

"No," she acknowledged. "I don't, but there are no guarantees, John, and I'm not asking for any…except that you love me."

"But I have nothing to offer you, dammit," he argued. "I messed up my life, lost everything. What do you think your family's going to think of me?"

"I didn't notice my brother objecting too strongly when I said I loved you," she pointed out. "And don't play the poor-me card. You're not some bum who wandered in off the street. You're a Navy SEAL who's been through a hell of a lot. And what do you mean…you have nothing to offer me? You have *you!* Don't you know how wonderful you are?"

"Maybe you need to talk to my ex-wife," he said dryly. "Trust me, by the time we divorced, she didn't think I was so wonderful."

"I'm sure it was a very difficult time for both of you," she replied. "You blamed yourself for something you couldn't have foreseen, then spent the next God-knows-how-many years punishing yourself."

"And that's what you want?"

Was he really so blind? Could he not see how special he was? Pushing to her feet, she stepped in front of him and took his hands in hers. Tears swam in her eyes as she looked up at him with a smile that came straight from her heart. "What I want is a man who realized what he was doing to himself and got help. I want a man who didn't give up when he lost everything. He went to work, instead. I want a man who knows his own weaknesses, who fought them and won. I want you. I love you."

"But I don't even have a home where I can take you."

"Do you think my family would have this ranch if someone hadn't given it to us? I'm not worried about what you do or don't have. Together, we can have whatever we want."

She made it sound so easy. "Elizabeth...please... it's not that simple."

"Why isn't it? I love you, and you love me. Nothing else matters, so don't even try to throw roadblocks in our way. I'm not losing you, and I'm not letting you lose me."

She had that determined look in her eyes, the one that warned him she was going to dig in her heels and fight for what she wanted and nothing he said or did was going to change her mind. And she wanted him.

Emotions flooded his heart, and for the first time since Mark died and his life spiraled down into a never-ending nightmare, he felt as if he could be the man he'd been before the accident. And it was all because of Elizabeth and her faith in him.

His fingers tightened around hers. "Do you know how incredible you are? Or how much I love you?"

Tears sparkled in her eyes. "If it's as much as I love you, then I'm one lucky woman."

"Oh, no, I'm the lucky one," he assured her. "And now that you've hit me over the head a couple of times and made me realize it, I'm not about to let you get away."

"So what are you going to do?" she teased, "hogtie me to your bed?"

"Maybe later," he said huskily. "But first I'm going to put a ring on your finger...if you say yes, of course. Will you marry me, Elizabeth? Will you build a life with me and have my children? Will you stay with me through thick and thin and grow old with me? I love you with all my heart. Say yes and you'll make me the happiest man on earth."

She didn't have to think, didn't even hesitate. Glowing with love, she threw herself into his arms. "Yes!"

On a distant hill, a man stood in the thick shadows cast by the towering pines and lifted high-powered binoculars to his eyes. Training them on the couple locked in an embrace on the porch of the foreman's cabin, he swore roundly when the Wyatt bitch kissed Cassidy like there was no tomorrow.

Obviously, she wasn't going back to London as she'd planned.

Stupid broad, he thought grimly. Let her stay. It wouldn't change anything. He was still going to inherit the Broken Arrow, and there wasn't a damn thing she or any of the Wyatts could do to stop him. He'd make damn sure of it.

Epilogue

Standing in the open doorway of the pantry, Elizabeth studied the contents of the shelves and couldn't stop smiling. John loved her. She still couldn't believe it. She wanted to shout it to the heavens, dance on a cloud, sing with the wind. Instead, she was making dinner to celebrate her and John's engagement and Buck and Rainey's homecoming, and she didn't have a clue what she was going to cook. It had to be something wonderful, she told herself, only to laugh at the idea. What difference did it make? She was so excited, she probably wouldn't taste it anyway!

Grinning at the thought as her gaze landed on a can of tuna, she could just imagine what everyone would say if she served tuna casserole tonight. John would—

"Gotcha!"

With no more warning than that, John came up behind her and slipped a blindfold over her eyes. "John!" she laughed. "What are you doing?"

"Kidnapping you," he chuckled. "No, no," he added, quickly catching her hands before she could pull the blindfold off. "No peeking. I have a surprise for you."

"What kind of surprise?"

"Wait and see," he chuckled, and took her hand. "C'mon. I'll show you."

Giggling, she blindly let him lead her out of the kitchen and outside, only to stop short when she heard him open a car door. "Where are we going?"

"Just for a little ride, sweetheart. Watch your head. That's it."

"John—"

He chuckled at her warning tone. "Where's your sense of adventure? Trust me, you'll be pleasantly surprised."

"I'm going to hold you to that," she told him as he buckled her seat belt for her. "If this is some kind of joke, I'm making tuna casserole for dinner!"

"Did I happen to mention that I love tuna casserole," he laughed. "You need to know that since we're getting married."

"If you live that long," she retorted, trying to scowl beneath her blindfold and failing miserably. "Where *are* we going?"

"Just hold your horses. We're almost there."

He didn't know what he was asking of her. She wasn't good at surprises. She couldn't stand not knowing. While he was driving, she'd just sneak a peek—

"Don't you dare!"

She giggled, her fingers closing around his as he grabbed her hand. "You're no fun at all."

"Just behave yourself and we'll get along fine," he said dryly, grinning. When she just sniffed, he just kept driving.

Thirty minutes later she was tapping her foot when he finally braked to a stop and cut the engine. "Okay," the told her. "You can take off the blindfold."

Whatever Elizabeth was expecting to see, it wasn't the cabin where they'd both nearly been killed. The damage from the fire was stark in the late-afternoon light. Her smile fading, she frowned up at John confusion. "This is your surprise?"

"Mmm-hmm," he said easily as he settled more comfortably in his seat and took her hand once again. "I had a long talk with Buck. We worked out a deal."

With his fingers wrapped around hers and his thumb rubbing back and fourth against the palm of her hand, she found it nearly impossible to concentrate. "About what?" she asked, trying to focus.

"The herd," he replied. "I was hired to build it back up, you know. Buck promised to give me one calf for every four that are born so I can build up my own herd."

"He did? You're kidding!"

"I said the same thing," he said with a smile, "But he was damn serious. By the time the year is up and your family has a free-and-clear title to the ranch, I'm going to have a sizable herd of my own."

She frowned. "So what are you saying?"

"Just that with the sale of some of the cattle—and the money I'm able to save from my salary—I'll have enough money to remodel the cabin and add electricity. I thought we could use the original cabin as our bedroom and build on around it. If that's what you want. Of course, if you'd rather live in the main house with your family—"

"No!"

"—I'll just tell Buck thanks but no, thanks. I'm sure he'll understand."

"No!" she cried. "This is perfect!"

"Are you sure?" he asked with pretended innocence. "We can build somewhere else on the property. You're one-fourth owner. Buck said pick out a spot."

If she hadn't seen the twinkle in his eye, she never would have realized he was teasing. He wanted to restore the cabin as much as she did. "Wretch!" she growled, laughing as he reached for her. "Don't you dare!"

"Whatever you say, sweetheart. You're the boss."

* * * * *